Detached

Detached

THE MYSTIC CHRONICLES
A HAMLET RETELLING

BRIGIT ROSÉ

To my fans.

None of this would be possible without your wonderful support.
I'm grateful every day that I get to do what I love and
I look forward to providing you with more stories.

Terminology

Hunter – a term used to describe a human with extraordinary abilities (hearing, speed, and sight) that kill otherworldly creatures including vampires, witches, and shapeshifters

Faun – a term used to describe a hunter on their first solo hunt of a vampire, witch, or shapeshifter

Shapeshifter – a term used to describe one of five bloodlines with the ability to turn into a large animal at will (Feline, Lupine, Ursidae, Leporidae, or Lacertidae)

Vampire – a term used to describe a human that has transitioned into an otherworldly creature with extraordinary abilities either by birth or death

Clan – identifies a group of vampires with common attributions; there is a total of seven in existence

Newling – a term used to describe a vampire who is within the first few years of their transition

Élan Clan – a group of vampires who value intellect and honor above all else

VēlM Clan – a group of vampires who value emotion, beauty, and art above all else

Katára Clan – a group of vampires who were turned by dying with vampire blood in their system

Vampire Council – consists of one member from each of the seven clans; it is believed these are the oldest and strongest vampires alive

one

"PAPA, I'M FINE," ODESSA PRACTICALLY yelled into her cell phone. Not that she meant to, even if her father deserved it. He'd convinced her this move would be good and *now* he wanted her to come home. What backwards thinking had her father gotten into?

"I don't believe it. The news talked about another murder that happened there. A young woman about your age. Pack everything up. You're coming home."

She let out an exasperated sigh. "And what would I tell my new job? How would that look if I just up and left without a word?"

"I don't care. I should've never let Claude talk me into this."

"Claude?" she snapped. "Why would you have spoken to him about me?" Of all the men in her late fiancé's family, she trusted his uncle the least. He reminded her of a sniveling weasel. He'd always looked for a way into someone's pocket. In her opinion, anyway.

"I didn't know what else to do," her father replied. "I'd stood by as your mother succumbed to that disease. After Hamilton's death… I know it was hard on you, but I saw the signs, Odessa. It wasn't something I could do again."

A shiver ran down her spine. Although her father didn't reference the signs, she knew what they were—seeing and hearing things that didn't exist. It hadn't mattered that her therapist reminded her she simply conjured memories of the time she and Hamilton had together. "I know, Papa."

"I'm sorry if it bothers you. I just… I thought Claude might understand my predicament. And the last thing I wanted was to make things harder on anyone, especially you or Gladys."

Yeah. Hamilton's mother wouldn't have been a good option. The female had taken Hamilton's death worse than she had. Though it made sense. He was Gladys's only son. Odessa rubbed her arm to staunch the sudden chill that swept through her body. "I understand. I just wish you would've told me. That you felt you could trust me enough to share your thoughts with me."

"It had nothing to do with a lack of trust, sweetheart. You simply… you weren't in a good head space. Besides, you seem positive all has worked out well. Though, I still think you should come home. You're too green to be out there all alone."

And now they'd gone full circle. At least something hadn't changed. Though she'd only left home a few days ago. A breeze blew through the living room and ruffled the hem of her blouse. Except that wasn't possible. She'd closed all the windows in her apartment. It wasn't yet winter, but the temperature dropped a bit at night. "What did Claude say to you, Papa?" Odessa strode down the hallway. Stopping in her bedroom doorway, she glanced at the window. What in the world? How had it gotten open? Hadn't she closed it?

"When? You mean when I asked for his opinion?"

"Of course." Why would she care about anything else? She rolled her eyes as she crossed her bedroom, stepping around the shoes she'd left on the floor. Odessa shut the window and locked it. Maybe she'd forgotten to do that before. It could've flown open by accident. To be sure, she'd mention it to maintenance and have them look at it.

"He suggested I let you move. Even recommended a few different cities that might be adequate."

"Including New York?" she clarified. Given her father's penchant for excluding information, it was best she be direct. But if this was Claude's idea, what had he gotten out of it? She was fairly certain he still lived in Solvang.

"Well, yes, but all the places he suggested had renowned libraries. It only made sense you go someplace that worked for you and gave you a fresh start."

Of course. Leave it to her late-fiancé's uncle to think of those things. Her initial question still stood—why? What did Claude get out of all of this? Not something she could ask her father directly. At least, not without rousing suspicion. Although, perhaps she simply needed to come at it from a different direction. "Well, rest-assured, despite what you see on the news, New York is perfectly safe. I'm sure you can confirm that with Claude the next time you see him."

"It may be some time before that happens."

"Which part?" Her father wouldn't rest soon. Of that, she was certain, especially with the distance between them. He'd always worried too much about her. Odessa peered out her window, but didn't notice anything out of the ordinary. Nothing that would cause unrest, anyway. Even at this time of night, the street below bustled with traffic, both cars and people strolling toward home.

"You're my treasure. I'll never stop worrying about you, but that's beside the point. Claude is away on business, so I'll have to speak with him when he returns."

Away on business, she thought to herself. Why didn't that news surprise her? Not that it meant he'd made his way to New York. Even if the male had, that could be nothing more than a coincidence. Odessa shook her head, spun on her heel, and started toward the living room. This was what her therapist had called an overactive imagination. She linked things together that simply made no sense. And this was one of them. "Can't you just trust what I'm telling you, Papa? You have nothing..." her words trailed off as she entered the living room and a gust of wind blew across the flap of a box.

What the hell?

Her gaze flicked to the window to the right of the couch. Something weird was definitely going on. She was damn sure she'd shut that window. What if someone had broken in? Oh God. It was possible. Her father had mentioned that female he'd heard about. "I'll call you back, Papa," she muttered. Before he could argue with her, she hung up the phone and pressed 9-1-1 on her cell phone. Better to be prepared to dial than to overreact. Shit. Did she have anything handy that she could protect herself with, just in case? Odessa scanned the area by her entertainment center and noticed the bat she hadn't yet put away.

She picked it up, got as good a grip as she could without letting go of her cell phone, and surveyed the living room. Nothing looked out of place. Although she still had a lot to unpack, all the boxes appeared to be exactly where she'd left them. Could someone have snuck into her apartment without knocking anything over? Not likely.

Slowly, Odessa crossed the room with the bat still at the ready as she headed toward the window. A scraping sound came from the kitchen. She glanced over her shoulder. Not that she could see much of anything. The light in the living room didn't project that far. A shiver shot down her spine. What if someone lurked in the shadows? What the fuck would she accomplish with a bat? Maybe… maybe it would be enough to scare them off.

Her stomach rolled. If not… no, she couldn't go there. Her father wouldn't survive if anything happened to her. Nor would she ever hear the end of it. Okay. She could do this. She could check out the noise. Odessa swallowed to wet her parched throat. It could just be her mind playing tricks on her. Only one way to find out. Turning around, she inched toward to the kitchen and strode around the kitchen island.

Meow.

"Jesus!" Odessa dragged a hand down her face and lowered the bat as she stared at the tiny black kitten. Yeah. She'd lost her mind alright. "How did you get in here?" With a shake of her head, she set the bat aside, crouched down on the back of her haunches, and scooped the small fluff ball into her arms. It couldn't be more than a couple of months old. "Let's get the window shut and I'll see what I have around here to feed you."

Maybe she had a can of tuna or something. Could she give him or her that? Her father hadn't ever allowed her a pet growing up, so she had little knowledge of what they could eat. She'd do a quick search on her cell. She strolled over to the window, closed it, locked it, and raised an eyebrow. Odessa swept her finger across the side where it locked and eyed the white powder on her finger pad. It almost looked like paint dust or something from the locking mechanism. Maybe it would be best if she found a couple of pieces of wood to ensure the windows remained shut. At least for tonight. Her gaze flicked from the outside world to the kitten.

"You know, I just moved in, but I wouldn't mind a companion. I'll have to give you a name. How about… Bard?" While he ate, she could call her father back. Hopefully, he hadn't imagined the worst and overreacted. Though knowing her father, the first likely applied. She might stop the second from happening.

Hamilton scanned over the text in the tome for the third time tonight. Not that the words appeared any different from the first time he'd read it. Just like it had for the last few weeks. How many days had he come to the library? And researched the same thing repeatedly? It got him nowhere.

He'd known about vampires since birth. It shouldn't be this difficult to find a way to reverse this… disease. There had to be one, except no matter how many tomes he scoured, he couldn't find a single reference to a cure. He surveyed the ancient texts he had scattered across the table. Maybe he needed to search grimoires. Not that they'd have anything like that in the library. Even here, where he could procure anything his heart desired. But there might be something to point him in the right direction.

Getting to his feet, Hamilton strode toward the preservation room. He already had a few tomes out from there and he couldn't spend all night looking through them. At least not the more fragile texts. Those he had to handle with extreme care. He rounded the corner, inputted the security code for the door, and let himself in.

He glanced around the room and ran a hand across the top of his head. Where did he start? The glass cases or those books stacked upon the shelves. Which would provide him a small clue as to answers he sought? They were each sorted by rarity, region, and age. The cases held the older books, so it seemed like the best option.

Hamilton strolled across the room and stopped in front of the case closest to the door. He eyed the leather-bound covers around each of the three books. A quick assessment of the hieroglyphs etched into the covers told him all he needed to know. Each book came from Egypt, somewhere around 5th century B.C. Nothing he ascertained from them would be useful. He moved onto the next case.

His ears perked at the crescendo of creaks as someone approached from the direction he'd come. From the sound of the footsteps and those high-end shoes, it could only be one person. His gaze flicked toward the door. Not a moment later, he spotted his sire through the glass. Hamilton let out a heavy sigh and returned his attention to the tomes inside the case in front of him.

"Why does it not surprise me I find you in here again?" Theo asked.

"That seems like a redundant question." One to which the male already knew the answer. They'd had this conversation far more times than he cared to think about.

"You know good and well you'll not find that which you seek. Why do you insist on this fruitless endeavor?"

Hamilton glowered at his sire. He despised the male and his fancy clothes. Not that they had much of anything to do with how he felt about the situation. They just reminded him every day of what he'd become.

"You know damn well why. Do you really need me to remind you again?"

"Your insistence on the impossible doesn't mean a cure exists. Do you not think if it did, one might've discovered it in the centuries that vampires have existed?" Theo took a few steps forward and clasped his hands at the small of his back. "It is well beyond time you accept your new station in life, Hamilton."

"Accept?" he snapped. "I was a hunter, and you turned me into a monster."

"I saved your life!" Theo retorted. "Or have you forgotten that?"

"That's what you call this? A life where I have to feed to survive? What kind of life is that?" Hamilton sneered. "And let's not forget that *you* chose to turn me. I didn't ask for this." Nor would he ever have asked for it. Hunters died with dignity. At least most did. Theo hadn't extended him that courtesy. Not that the male had ever disclosed why he'd turned him. That wasn't entirely true. He just didn't believe the answers provided.

"You complain and retort about the life I've given you, yet you continue on this mission day after day. If you truly believe death to be the better option, then take that path. No one is stopping you."

Hamilton narrowed his eyes and scoffed. The male would suggest that. He didn't want to be a vampire. No, he wanted his life back. The one so graciously stolen from him. Shaking his head, he returned his attention to the encased books.

"That's what I thought." Theo smirked. "Ensure you clean up your mess, Hamilton. No one here must know of our presence." The male turned on his heel and started for the door.

He flicked his gaze to his sire's back. "You act all high and mighty and as if I should be grateful for what you've given me, but if that were the truth, then why haven't you presented me to the council?" A question he'd posed before. Not that he'd ever gotten a straight answer.

"I will present you to them when the time is right."

"Right. Of course, you will." Hamilton folded his arms across his chest. "And I'm sure that'll include that I'm not like any other human." Yeah, he didn't believe that for one second.

Theo spun around and faced him. The male's eyes darkened as he took a step toward Hamilton. "I cannot present you to them until you've learned to accept your new life. Instead of attempting to discover all the abilities that come with it, you waste and fritter away your time searching for something that doesn't exist. Regardless of how many times I tell you this. As for your previous status, allow them to discover it. Tell them. But know that if you do, everyone you may still care about from your prior life will cease to exist. Their deaths will be on your hands. Not that it'll be the end. The council will then turn you into one of their dancing monkeys as they take every bit of knowledge you have regarding hunters to rid us of their existence. By the time they finish with you, nothing will remain except a shell of who you once were. And you'll be powerless to stop them." He stopped in front of him. "Despite what you may think of me, Hamilton, every decision I make is to protect you. But continue down this path. Obviously, you know better than I." Theo waved a dismissive hand at Hamilton, clicked his heels together, turned around, and walked out of the preservation room.

He stared at the space where his sire had once stood. What the fuck was he supposed to make of all that? It was the most the male had ever said at one time. Did that mean Theo had a point? Yes, he'd figured out some of his abilities, but he didn't know all of them. Would him being born a hunter make a difference? Would the council really pry his knowledge of hunters from him? If they discovered that, would they really go after his loved ones? His mother? His ex… God, he couldn't even think about that. He dragged a hand down his face, dropped his eyes to the glass case, and stared at his reflection.

The face of someone he didn't even know anymore looked back at him. A male who once put everyone he loved before himself. Now… he only thought about himself. And getting back to them. Instead of the male his father had raised him to be. He hated everything he'd become. Hamilton punched the case. Glass shattered all around his fist and scattered across the books. Blood beaded on his skin.

"Damn it," he mumbled. He didn't care about the mess he'd made of his hand. It would quickly heal. But now he had to clean this up, get it all fixed, and return home before the sun rose. Letting out a sigh of exasperation, he gripped the back of his neck. He had his work cut out for him, but it would give him time to think. Because something had to change. And soon.

Two

ODESSA PEERED AT THE FEMALE showing her around the library out of the corner of her eye. A tour made sense for her first night. Though she certainly hadn't expected it to take this long for them just to cover the first floor. Together, the two of them headed up the staircase toward the second floor. The clack of their high heels echoed around them with each step they took. This time of night, the library was completely empty, save for the two of them.

Aside from Laura's voice, the only noises she'd noted over the last hour comprised the ticking of a clock. At least she didn't have to deal with the bustling of children and other book patrons. Those would come with the few day shifts she had scheduled over the coming weeks. Though she preferred the quiet, she could handle the noise when necessary.

She stopped at the top of the staircase and surveyed the bookshelves curling around various reading nooks and study areas and lining the walls. Drinking it all in, Odessa took in a deep breath. The sweet scent of crisp paper and dust filled her nostrils. Oh, what a glorious smell. Something she'd certainly missed back home. This place was far more extensive. Taking a few steps forward, she eyed the paintings along the walls.

Her gaze landed on a portrait hanging high above the others. It couldn't be. She had to be seeing things. Or over-analyzing the portrait. Slowly walking toward it, she studied the male's features—his strong jawline, hunter-green eyes, and dark, wavy hair. If she didn't know any better, she'd almost swear he looked exactly like her late fiancé. That couldn't be. Odessa glimpsed over her shoulder at Laura and pointed to the portrait. "Who's that?"

"Oh, that's our benefactor… well, owner, Hamilton Morck."

Odessa's head snapped back to the dark-haired female. "I'm sorry. Could you repeat his name?" Because she had to have heard that wrong. No way this male not only looked like her fiancé, but shared the same first name.

"Hamilton Morck. No one has really seen him. The only one I know who even communicated with him was our previous conservator. Most of us just know he's a wealthy benefactor and we wouldn't have the lower floors without him. They definitely require someone like you."

Right. The conservator position. If they truly purchased rare items, they hadn't gotten their hands on before; it made sense. She glanced back at the portrait. Her late fiancé simply had a doppelgänger. That was the only plausible explanation. A shiver shot down her spine. Odessa shuddered. Strange. She shook off the sensation and flicked her gaze back to Laura. "Well, why don't we head toward the lower levels, then? I'm sure you're ready to head home."

"Of course." The female gestured to the nearby elevator.

They strode toward it, bypassing the staircase. As much as she hadn't minded the ascension to the second level, they had two levels below to cover. That seemed like an awful lot. She peered back at the portrait of Hamilton Morck. Another shiver shot through her body. Work, she needed to get to that. Odessa turned her attention to Laura. "You could just show me the preservation room and maybe where all the supplies are so I can get started on things. I mean, if that works for you."

Laura grinned. "I can see you're eager to work. Yeah. I can do that. If need be, we can always pick up on the tour tomorrow night."

"That sounds good." It was easy enough to agree to. She had few problems in the past finding her way around libraries. Even if this was the largest she'd ever worked at, it wouldn't matter. She could find her way around with ease. The elevator door slid open. They entered it and both turned around, facing the portrait one last time. Her gaze remained focused on it until the elevator door closed.

"Hard to look away, isn't it? I don't blame you. He's quite a handsome man."

"You said you've never met him, right? Do you… know anything about him?" Why was she even asking this? *That* man in the painting wasn't her Hamilton.

"Honestly, no. I'm not even sure he exists."

Odessa frowned. "What do you mean?" How was that possible? The library had a painting of him. Unless someone had painted a fictional person, which she supposed was plausible. Artists created things all the time. Not that she'd even bothered to see who'd done the portrait.

"I did an internet search a few months back. Nothing comes up, which is odd. Most people you can find something."

Not necessarily. Very little came up if anyone searched her name. She only had a professional profile out there. Nothing else. "Maybe he's just a private person," Odessa replied as the elevator door opened, letting them out onto the bottom floor.

"That's true." The two of them exited the elevator and headed to the right. "We have rows of books on either side of the preservation room, which is in the middle. Plus, there are tables around the corner where people can review the books. Those that don't require the steady temperature are on these shelves."

Which made perfect sense. "What about wash areas?" She suspected there had to be a couple of those around since it had become recommended that people handle older and rare books with clean hands versus gloves. Only certain items required those.

"There's one on each end."

"Excellent." They rounded the corner and her eyes landed on a group of open texts spread out across a nearby table. She pointed them out. "Is that common?" While she couldn't tell the age of the books from where they stood, she could see they appeared older.

"No."

"The library's empty, right?" That's what the female had told her upon her arrival. She strode up to the table, eyed the various tomes, and held her hand out to stop Laura from touching them. "These are all fairly old. I'd say around 5th century B.C." Odessa stepped to the right and lingered over one book. "I've seen this one before."

"Oh?"

"Yes, but it was in a museum." She peered at Laura. How did they have this? Unless it wasn't the same book. Maybe she'd mistaken it. She turned her attention to the open page and scanned over the writings.

"Hamilton!" she half-whispered and yelled as she waved him over from the painting her fiancé still stood in front of. "Come look at this."

"What?" he asked as he joined her and slipped a hand around her waist.

"Look." Odessa pointed to the book. It was the entire reason she'd wanted to visit this museum. A place she never thought she'd get him. He'd never cared for them. One of many reasons their time here meant so much to her. "It's 5th century B.C. Written in Latin talking about the first appearance of mythological creatures." Not that they could see a lot. The museum only had the book open to the first few pages.

Her fiancé stiffened a bit behind her. He cleared his throat. "Um, that's interesting."

This book also contained Latin passages. She could see that much from the text. Though the page in front of her spoke of witches and spells. No way she could be certain if this was the same book. Odessa glanced over her shoulder and located the hand-washing station in the back corner. "Let me wash my hands before picking those up and returning them to the preservation room. They can't remain open like this. It could damage the spine."

"Of course. Is there anything I can do to help?"

"Can you do a sweep of the other side and make sure nothing else is out?" That would tell her if she had to handle anything else. And keep them from wasting time if it was empty.

"Sure." With a dip of her chin, Laura disappeared down the hallway.

She imagined that passed right by the preservation room. Odessa strode over to the wash-station. It made sense to keep it away from books. This way, nothing got damaged. Provided no pipes burst. She'd suggest they prepare for any possibility of that occurring.

Odessa turned the water on, got some of the soap on her hands, and scrubbed them for a good thirty seconds. She sniffed the foam covering her hand. Good. No extra scent. Just plain, anti-bacterial soap. Once she had them rinsed off, she retrieved a paper towel, dried her hands, and shut off the faucet. Better to use the paper towel in her palm, then to undo the washing. As she dried the last of the water from her hands, she heard someone muttering. It sounded masculine, but that wasn't possible.

She listened intently. Silence greeted her. Shaking her head, Odessa threw away the paper towel. She returned to the table and carefully turned the pages of the one tome. Sure enough, it was the book she'd seen in the museum. How had they gotten their hands on it?

"There's nothing on the other side," Laura said as she approached the table.

With a slight nod, Odessa shut the book all the way. She half turned toward the female. "Did you say something a few minutes ago?"

"No. Why?"

The last thing she wanted to admit was the truth. No reason to give anyone any ammunition that could make them think she was crazy. The night before had already done a number on her with the windows. But lying seemed like a bad habit to form with a new job. "I just thought I heard something, but it was probably the pipes."

"Um, yeah. So, are you ready to head to the preservation room?"

That didn't sound comforting. Too late to take the admission back now. "Yes." She picked up the tome closest to her and followed Laura down the hall and around the corner. From their current position, she spotted the other tables and remaining bookcases. This place certainly had an extensive collection. Her gaze shifted to the keypad by the door to the preservation room.

"The code is two-oh-one-eight."

"Easy enough to remember." Cute. They'd set it to the current year. Also simple. She'd recommend that get changed. Best way to prevent theft. Odessa entered the room after Laura. She stopped just inside and took in her surroundings. The room comprised four display cases and long bookcases against each wall. At least someone stored all the books correctly. Small to medium-sized books stood upright. Most shelves contained books of the same size. The display cases appeared to hold the larger books, amongst other materials. Lighting in the room remained low. She inhaled deeply. The papery smell of old books and leather filled her nostrils. God, this brought back so many wonderful memories.

A shiver shot down her spine. It was like an icy blast or something just hit her, which was strange. This room had perfect ventilation for the items it held. Likely, it was just her imagination. Shaking it off, she cleared her throat. "Um, let me get this put up and then you can show me the supply closet."

"Are you sure you don't want me to take you on the rest of the tour? I really don't mind."

"No, thank you. I'd just like to get to work." Work would wash whatever had crept over her away. It had worked in the past. Anytime her thoughts wandered, work pulled her out of it. She simply needed tasks to focus on and she could see the cleaning that required her attention.

Odessa located the display case where this tome belonged. It was unlocked. Yeah, because that was safe. Millions of dollars' worth of ancient texts and it seemed like anyone could access them. Something else to discuss with the manager. They needed better security protocols in place.

"Alright. Come with me." Laura led her out of the preservation room, around the corner, and down the hall. The female opened the closet and gestured to the shelves full of various tools, including brushes of different sizes, steel micro-spatulas, tweezers, scalpels, Teflon and bone folders, magnifying glasses, and more. "Everything you could need."

"I see that." It meant she didn't have to provide anything herself, which she'd done in the past. Those jobs she never stayed at long. They asked for too much and paid too little. This place definitely didn't fit those standards. "Close it. I won't get anything yet. Not until I get the rest of the books put up."

"Sure thing." The female shut the closet. "Is there anything else you need before I go?" Laura asked as they headed toward the other side of the building, back to the table.

"No. Nothing that I can think of." And that was the truth. The continued tour seemed highly unnecessary. Laura had shown her the location of all the important stuff. She stopped at the table, carefully closed two more books, and collected them in her arms. "Have a good night, Laura. Thank you for everything tonight."

"You're welcome. You do the same," the female replied and continued on to the elevator with a small wave over her shoulder.

The latter went without saying. Her passion for her work ensured she'd have a wonderful evening. Odessa headed back to the preservation room. All the books left out on the table belonged in there. These went on a shelf. Not that she was sure which one yet. But she suspected it wouldn't take long for her to figure out the right one.

Odessa paused in front of the door to the preservation room long enough to enter the entry code. She pushed the door open, stepped into the room, and strode over to the shelves against the far wall. Given the book sizes, it seemed like the most appropriate place to start. She scanned the different shelves and discovered the right one, after a few minutes, for the first book. With that in place, she walked to the opposite side of the room.

God, there were so many shelves. This one wouldn't be as easy as the other one. It was smaller than the others, but thick. What kind of information did it hold? She had all night for work. It wouldn't hurt anyone if she took a peek. Odessa opened the tome and surveyed a few of the pages. "Hmm. Vampires." Not something she expected, but it certainly interested her. The pages contained information on one of the many origins that existed.

"Odessa?" a familiar voice called out.

Her head jerked in its direction. She dropped the book in her hands. It couldn't be. "Hamilton?" Odessa whispered. Oh, God. How had she conjured him up in her mind? The image looked so real. Then it disappeared. She shook her head and gripped the bookcase.

This wasn't happening again. It couldn't be happening. Not here. She'd left all the terrible memories and her past behind. This was a place for her to start over. She rubbed her eyes. "No. You can't be here. I'm not seeing you," Odessa said aloud. She had to say the words. Just like she'd done before. She couldn't truly clear the image from her mind otherwise. Inhaling and exhaling a few times, she concentrated on the breath in her lungs. Every step she'd taken in the past to free her mind from the illusion of all she missed.

With one final deep breath, Odessa crouched down and picked up the book. She returned to finding the right spot for the tome. Work would help keep this from occurring **again**. Or so she hoped.

Hamilton opened the door to the manor, stalked through the foyer, and headed straight for their dining room. Aside from their wet bar out by the pool, it was the only place that had a decanter of alcohol. After what he just discovered, he needed a stiff drink. He stormed over to the small wet bar to the left of the large dining room table. It was big enough to seat ten people. Not that they ever had guests.

As he poured himself a glass of bourbon, he heard the front door shut.

Hamilton chugged half the glass back. Unlike most turned vampires, he could drink and eat. Almost as if nothing had changed with his digestive system. From what he'd read, this was something that typically only born vampires could do. None of that mattered at the moment. He glanced over his shoulder. The click of his sire's shoes echoed against the mansion's wooden floors.

"Would you care to explain what that was all about?" Theo questioned as he entered the room.

"Which part?" Hamilton knocked the last of the bourbon in his glass back and poured himself another. He dragged a hand across the top of his head. This couldn't have happened. No way had he just seen his ex-fiancée. Regardless of how many times he replayed that scenario in his head, it didn't change the outcome.

Hamilton inputted the entry code to the preservation room. He'd left his sire back in the other room. The male had gone off too many times about his research. It annoyed him how often he heard the same lecture. He opened the door and stopped just in the doorway. "Odessa?"

She jerked her head toward him, dropped the book she held, and uttered his name. A jolt of lightning ran through him as he drank in the sight of his love. Her long, blonde hair hung down, now half-way down her back. It hadn't been that long last year. Maybe midway, as he recalled. What was she doing here in New York? It didn't make a bit of sense, yet there she stood, less than ten feet from him.

Shit. She could see him. It hadn't even occurred to him when he first spotted her. Hamilton went invisible as his sire approached behind him. He glanced over his shoulder, but the male had gone invisible, too. Oh, God. What she must be thinking?

Fuck. After his death, he'd tried so hard to stay away from her. Though he'd secretly watched over her, nothing like this had ever happened. How the hell was he going to avoid her now?

"Don't play dumb, Hamilton. You knew that female. The blonde. Who is she?"

He smirked. Interesting that the male asked when just last night Theo threatened him with what the council would do. Hamilton chugged half the second glass of bourbon. "Her name is Odessa Black. She is… was… my fiancée."

Theo pinched the bridge of his nose. "Please tell me you're joking."

"Do you seriously think this is something I'd joke about?" He'd left her over a year ago to mourn his death. The one person whom he loved most in the world, aside from his mother. Even that woman had her moments, especially after she'd married his uncle mere months after his father's death. Nothing about this seemed right.

"What is she doing here? At the library, no less?"

Hamilton drank the last of the bourbon in his glass and faced his sire. "I'd say she's the new conservator. That is what she has a degree for. And the death of the last one kind of opened up a position." Yeah, he was still sour about that.

"That doesn't really answer the question. Why here? Why this library? We'll need to find out."

"Exactly how do you intend to do that?" Because he'd be damned if anyone endangered her life. He may be a vampire, but that didn't mean he couldn't do everything in his power to protect her from this world. Something he'd done since the day they met.

"The library would've done a background check and application. I'll have someone go through her place, see what they find."

"Absolutely not! No one goes near her, except me. She's my responsibility." And he'd do whatever it took to keep her safe. Even if she didn't know about it.

"You need to stay away from her," Theo replied. "I'll handle everything. You'll do nothing. Do you understand me? Nothing." He left the dining room.

To hell with that. Odessa needed protection, and he didn't trust anyone else to offer it right. Thankfully, he had access to the library administrative systems from here. Something he hadn't shared with his sire. Hamilton strode out of the dining room and headed up the staircase to the second story. He had everything he required in his bedroom.

Odessa ascended the staircase, leaving the musk of stagnant water and mildew behind. She inhaled and exhaled a deep breath as she reached the top step. God, the air smelled so much fresher out here. She didn't think she'd ever get accustomed to the scents that accosted her on the subway, but it was the easiest way to travel. She refused to subject herself to the New York City taxi system. Nor would she ever drive a car in this city. There was far too much traffic for her liking.

A breath of silence greeted her. This time of morning, many were just waking up. Although there were some on the road, most of the streets remained quiet. One thing she loved about her shift. She started toward home, noting the many lights flooding the various tall brick buildings along each side of the street. Lights even shone through windows of some storefronts. Things were only beginning to come to life.

It would be interesting to see how everything changed when winter came. Would there be any snow on the ground? If so, how much? Would restaurants open later? Or start just as early? And what about traffic? Would it become even more clogged than it did presently? So many things to discover about this city. And she couldn't wait.

A slight shuffle of footsteps behind her caught her attention. Odessa glanced over her shoulder and shoved her hands deeper into her coat pockets. Hadn't she seen him on the subway? It was difficult to tell. The male wore a hat and kept it low over his face. She couldn't see enough to determine if it was the same person. What reason would anyone have to follow her?

It had to be her imagination. Maybe something left over from the chaos over the last couple of nights. Just in case, she focused on the sidewalk in front of her and picked up her pace. It seemed smarter than taking a chance. Might even be wise to locate the pepper spray in her purse. Provided she could get to it.

As discreetly as possible, she reached into her purse and wrapped her fingers around the pepper spray she kept on hand. The person's pace behind her increased, matching her own. What the fuck? He was seriously following her. Damn it. Alright. No big deal, right?

She'd reach her building in a couple of blocks. Although she had on heels, she could walk a little faster. Once she got inside, then she'd be safe. They had security at the front desk. She just had to get there. Without tripping over her own two feet. Odessa glanced over her shoulder as she hit the block of her building. The person had picked up their pace again.

Her heart raced, and her limbs shook. She had to do something. But what? She only had one option. To keep space between them, she bolted across the street, down the sidewalk, and ran up the staircase to her building. She yanked the door open, peered over her shoulder, and slammed right into someone.

"Whoa," the male said. "Are you okay?"

"No," she replied between heavy breaths. Odessa flicked her eyes to him briefly and looked back toward the door. "Someone's chasing me!"

"Frederick, call the police!" the man hollered.

"Yes, sir, Mr. Watson."

He gripped her arms. "Hey, look at me. You're alright. You're safe."

The hold he had on her did nothing to stop her body from trembling. Or the tears that welled in the corners of her eyes. She couldn't stop glancing back and forth between him and the door. What if the person who followed her only wanted to learn what building she lived in? Or where she lived, period? Oh, God. Then she'd led him right to her building. Tears rolled down her cheeks as she flicked her gaze to the male in front of her. "I'm so sorry," Odessa hiccupped.

"You're okay. There's nothing to apologize for."

She didn't really know this man. Yeah, she'd seen him around the building once or twice over the weekend, and the doorman seemed to know him. Not that either affected her need to apologize. He appeared on his way out and she'd run right into him.

"Why don't I escort you up to your apartment? Frederick can tell the police where to go when they arrive. That'll give you a chance to settle and calm down before speaking with them."

Normally, she'd decline such an offer, but she didn't know if she could make it to her door without aid. Although the beating of her heart had eased a bit, it wasn't enough. And being alone didn't sound all that appealing at the moment. "Thank you."

"You're welcome."

Three

FROM ABOVE, HAMILTON WATCHED AS some person followed Odessa from the subway station. They had their hat dipped low, so he couldn't see much of their face. Though he had an excellent vantage point. He stood on top of a building. As much as he'd wanted to stay close to Odessa, he couldn't risk her spotting him. Or anyone else. So, he'd chosen the best point of view from where he expected to see her close to her building.

Although, now he wished he had taken the lower ground. Then he could take care of the problem. Especially since this couldn't be anyone Theo had sent. The male hadn't gotten anything set up prior to his departure from the manor. Unless his sire had accomplished it afterward, but he would've heard from him if that was the case. They had cell phones for a reason.

He noticed Odessa pick up her pace below, and the person following her did the same. Though, they'd kept some distance between themselves and Odessa. Strange. They didn't appear to have any intention of grabbing her, but he refused to chance it. He glanced ahead and noted the number of buildings between hers and his current location. If he needed to leap to the ground, then so be it. Best way to prepare for that was to get ahead a little.

Hamilton darted across the rooftop, leaped over the alley below, and rolled into a smooth landing on the next roof. He checked out the situation below. Odessa hadn't yet noticed the pace of the person behind her. Not that he expected it would take much longer. His fiancée was a smart woman.

Just as he'd done with the previous roof, he charged ahead, pushed off just before hitting the ledge of the building, and jumped over the dark silence below. As he leaped from one rooftop to another, he spotted Odessa increase her pace twice more until she was running into her building. Certain she was now safe, he focused his attention on the one who dared to follow her. They lingered for only a moment by the staircase leading into her building and then continued on. He watched as they rounded the corner and headed into an alleyway.

This was his chance.

He ran across the roof and used the two nearby lower buildings to jump down to the ground below. It had taken a little work, but he positioned himself in front of the other person. While he still couldn't make out the minute details of their face, he could at least identify the perpetrator as male. And he didn't bother with questions. Those could come later. He balled up his fist and punched the man, sending him flying a few feet back.

The perpetrator skidded to a stop and smirked. "I recommend you walk away."

"Not happening," Hamilton growled. Simultaneously, he and the male charged at one another. He swung his fist at the man's cheek, who dodged the hit. The guy's uppercut hit him square in the jaw and threw him across the alleyway. With a loud thud, his back hit a dumpster. As if the assault of rotting garbage wasn't bad enough, it took him a moment to shake off the sting between his shoulder blades.

How the hell had the guy done that? Aside from the obvious. The guy definitely wasn't human. No human he knew of could accomplish such a feat. He got to his feet, snarled, and hissed as he eyed the empty spot where the man had stood. What the fuck? Where the fuck had the guy gone? Hamilton glanced one way down the alley, and then the other. Except he didn't see anything other than a couple of large waste bins filled to the hilt with trash. He eyed the rooftops above, but didn't catch sight of the guy.

Someone who packed that kind of power and disappeared this quickly. It had to be a vampire. Why would a vampire follow Odessa? He eyed the time on his watch. Not that it was really necessary. Even without checking how long he had, he sensed the sun was close to rising. His cell phone rang. Without hesitation, he answered it. Seemed pointless to look. Only one person had this number. "I'll be home shortly," he stated.

"You should've been home an hour ago," Theo retorted. "Where are you?"

Yeah, like he was going to share that information with his sire. "Nowhere important. I'll be back soon." Before the male could utter anything else, Hamilton hung up. Despite all the questions running through his mind about the perpetrator, he didn't have time to scour the alleyway for any clues to the guy's identity.

Not that he intended to let it go. Night time would be here soon enough. Then he'd find out whatever he could. He'd search until he discovered the truth. No matter how long it took.

Odessa checked she had everything in her purse. The ordeal from this morning wouldn't deter her from going to work. She refused to let it affect her in the slightest. A soft meow to her right caught her attention. With a smile, she crouched down on the back of her haunches and stroked the top of Bard's head. "I agree. It would be great if there's no dramatic return home tomorrow morning."

Bard responded with a drawn-out meow and rubbed up against her leg. She scooped him up into her arms, holding him close as she rose to her feet. The doorbell rang. Odessa cocked an eyebrow at her kitten. "Hmm, wonder who that could be?" She strode over to the door, her heels clicking against the hard wood floor. A sound she loved almost as much as the musty smell of old books.

Removing the chain, she cracked the door open. Her eyes widened a touch. "Austin?" Of all the people to stop by, she didn't expect him. It wouldn't surprise her if her brother or father made a surprise visit, though. Hopefully, no time soon.

"Hi." He flashed a heart-stopping grin. "I hope I'm not interrupting anything."

"Um, sort of. I'm actually getting ready to head off for work." She supposed the kitten in her arm said otherwise.

"Oh. Well, I'd be happy to walk you downstairs, if that's alright?"

He'd been nice this morning, but was it the same now? Or was there something else going on? Maybe she was just reading into things. It wasn't like he'd asked her out or anything. This was just what friendly neighbors looked like. "Sure. Give me a second to grab my things."

"Of course. Take your time."

It would be rude of her to make him wait outside. Her father raised her better than that. "Do you want to come in while you wait?" She opened the door a little wider, giving him plenty of room.

"I'd love to." Dipping his chin at her, he stepped inside and peered around her apartment. "You have a beautiful place."

"Thank you." Although he'd seen Bard this morning, she hadn't actually let him into her apartment. It seemed too personal, given what happened this morning. She shut the door behind him and set the kitten down on the ground. "It won't take me long." Odessa strode past him, collected her coat from the hall closet, and slipped it on.

"How did everything go with the police earlier?"

"Nowhere, really. By the time they got here, I guess the person was long gone." She shrugged. It had taken a good portion of the day to convince herself it wasn't all in her head. Someone had chased her this morning. The police planned to check any cameras they could locate, but they couldn't do much else. Not that she said as much. Instead, once she had her coat on, she retrieved her purse.

"I'm sorry to hear that, Odessa. Maybe instead of taking the subway home tomorrow morning, take a taxi. It's certainly the safer way to travel."

"That's something I've considered." Not that she wanted to live like that. "At least for now. I'll eventually have to take the subway again. I don't want this to control my life." Things that had happened had already taken too much from her.

"Good. To both." He opened the door as she grabbed her house keys.

"Thank you." Two words she meant in more way than one. Was it wrong that she found him attractive? Or that some part of her wanted to run her fingers through his blond hair? Shaking the thoughts from her head, she locked her apartment as they left.

"Has anyone ever told you that you have a beautiful smile?"

"Oh, um…" How did she respond to that aside from gratitude? "Thank you. That's very kind of you." She hadn't heard anything like that in such a long time. It was something Hamilton used to tell her all the time. Which only reminded her of the loss she'd felt for the last year. But she couldn't reminiscence on that. Especially standing here around Austin. That was the past. Not her present.

"You're welcome."

They strolled down the carpeted hallway toward the elevator. She fidgeted with her keys and glimpsed him out of her periphery. It was the safest way to ensure he didn't notice anything off with her. Maybe she could offer an explanation before things went further. Not that she knew if she even wanted that. "I'm sorry if I'm a tad quiet. It's been…a long time since anyone complimented me."

Austin clasped his hands behind him. "Normally, I'd say that sounds awful, but I get the sense there's a story to go with it."

"It's not something I prefer to talk about." Too much pain accompanied those memories. At least the last days she had with Hamilton. Things she couldn't think about right then. "The past is in the past."

"I can understand that. Sometimes it's better when it stays there, especially if it's complicated." He depressed the down button on the elevator.

"Most people wouldn't agree with you. They'd say the past can tell people a lot about the kind of person someone is." It's something her father would say. Followed by she had nothing to be ashamed about. Not that she agreed with his assessment. But he didn't know all the details of those last days. The things she regretted.

"I think it has more to do with a person's actions than their words." The elevator door opened. He held a hand out, gesturing for her to go first.

Odessa let out a soft chuckle, liking his gentlemanly presentation. It seemed over the top, but if he was trying to garner her attention, it worked. She stepped into the elevator. "Can I ask you something?"

"Feel free. I'm an open book." He got on behind her and pressed the button for the first floor.

"Are you always this nice?" It might seem like an odd question, but she had to know if this was common or just for her. This morning, it seemed different. That appeared natural, but this…she didn't quite know how to explain it.

"Yes. I try to be polite to all my neighbors. Though I'd be lying if I didn't admit that I have some ulterior motives right now."

"Dare I ask?" That didn't bode well. However, he could've lied to her about it, which said something about his sincerity. Didn't it? Aside from her family and best friend, the last person she'd met like that was… Hamilton. She had to stop thinking about her late fiancé.

"When I saw you, over the weekend, moving in, I'd initially planned to engage in a friendly conversation with you. See what you were like, hoping that I could invite you to dinner." He got this sheepish look on his face. "But I came to check on you and make sure you were okay. Plus, ask you out. If you'd be interested."

"Um, wow." That was a good question. Truthfully, he was quite handsome. He stood tall, over six-feet for sure. With that head of blond hair and bright-blue eyes, not to mention the way the suit cut his frame, she'd be an idiot to decline. No one had caught her attention in such a long time. If nothing else, it would be nice to befriend someone.

"It's okay if you're not. I promise you won't hurt my ego."

"That's not it at all." Her history only served as an excuse. Over a year had gone by since Hamilton's death. Despite their last days together, he'd want her to be happy. Odessa smiled. "I'd love to join you for dinner, Austin."

"I'm glad to hear that." A lopsided grin crossed his face. "Is tomorrow night too soon? Or does another night work better for you?"

"Tomorrow night is perfect." She was off from the library, so it worked out. "Now, you'll have to correct me if it's too late or early, but does seven sound good?"

Austin chuckled. "Not from New York I take it?"

"Far from it." The busy lifestyle she noted at night was something she had to get accustomed to. Hours upon hours of horns blaring, people chattering, and all kinds of other noises. "I was born in a town that's a little quieter."

"Well, you can tell me all about it tomorrow night. I'll pick you up at seven." The elevator door opened to the first floor.

"I look forward to it." Giving him one last look, she strode out of the elevator and exited the building. Work called.

Hamilton selected a walnut-colored, three-piece, Sebastian Cruz tweed suit for the evening. It wasn't what he'd worn as a hunter, but it seemed fitting as a vampire. Not that he had much control over his clothing. His sire had certain rules about things of this nature. Still, he wore it all well.

He eyed the suit as he laid it out on his four-poster king-sized bed. So much of this life drove him crazy, but other things he enjoyed. Though he could deal without the fancy-ass décor of his bedroom. The swirls on the walls didn't bother him so much as the various statues of angels and gods did. Strange as all get out to see on a day-to-day basis.

His gaze flicked to the door as he tugged on his pants. Even with the carpeted hallway, he could hear his sire stride toward his room. This likely had something to do with the situation from early this morning. Yeah, he'd barely made it back to the manor before the sun rose, but ensuring Odessa had gotten home safely made it worth it.

"Come in," Hamilton called out. No point in drawing this out more than necessary.

The door opened as he shrugged on a white, button-down shirt. Theo entered and clasped his hands at the small of his back. "Where do you think you're going?"

"The only place that matters to me right now." That bit seemed self-explanatory as far as he was concerned. He strolled around to the small dresser beside the bed, opened the top drawer, and removed a set of gold cufflinks.

"You need to stay away from her, which includes the library. If you insist on continuing this research nonsense, then explore the texts here."

Hamilton scoffed. As if he hadn't already scoured what they had in the house. None of it had proven useful. It only left him with more questions than answers. "I can't stay away."

"This isn't a request. It isn't safe for you or her. The more you show up, the more likely she is to be pulled into our world."

"She already is!" he snapped. Darting over to where Theo stood, he shoved the man. Not that his sire budged more than a couple of inches. "A vampire followed her home last night! Would you know anything about that?"

"Calm yourself! This instant." Theo cleared his throat. "Now, explain to what you're referring."

"I watched someone trail her back to her building. She ran in and he lingered outside for a moment before heading around the corner to an alley. I attacked him. Not only did he take the hit like I was a damn fly, but when he punched back, it knocked me on my ass." It summed up the fight, even though it certainly felt so much worse than how he described.

Hamilton dragged a hand down his face and dropped it to his hip. "How does that even happen?"

"You are well aware how. Or need I remind you that age and training make a difference?" He took a few steps over to the long dresser and leaned against it. "Something to consider in this crusade of yours. What if a hunter had shown up? Or a shapeshifter? Do you think you would've fared better? Or are you willing to risk her life?"

Hamilton sighed heavily. Damn it. He hated his sire had a point. Odessa's life was at risk. Just him hanging around wasn't enough. Somehow, she'd already gotten drawn into his world. Not that he'd intended that. He gripped the back of his neck, laced his fingers together, and dropped his gaze to the floor. Something had to be done. Even as a hunter, he'd always protected her. She deserved nothing less. With a slight nod, more to himself, he lifted his eyes to Theo. "Then what do we do?"

"Continue this futile research if you must, but if you wish to keep her safe, then you must train. We have only just touched the surface of your abilities."

How many times had his sire said that? More than he dared to count. None of that mattered right now. He had to face the truth. Just because he'd died, it didn't mean his love for Odessa had. He'd always love her. "Fine, but I will see her home every day. It's that simple."

"Ensure you're home before the sun rises. I prefer not to have to deal with your ashes."

"Right."

four

"I DIDN'T KNOW THIS CITY was so beautiful," Odessa commented as she and Austin made their way to the restaurant. Even the building where the entrance was located was stunning. Full of bright lights and golden patterns. Unlike anything she'd ever seen before. That seemed to be the theme for the night. Outside the Rockefeller Center, as he called it, stood a gold statue of Titan Prometheus. Well, more below it, near a skating rink.

"There's a lot to see. Maybe I can take you to some of the more prominent places. If you'd like."

"I think that would be wonderful," she agreed without a second thought. It would be nice to have someone who knew the city better than she did to show her around. She might even find some places to tour regularly alone. Or that her best friend might join her on. Someone else to talk to about touring the city.

Austin smiled as they approached the hostess outside the door of the restaurant. "Two," he said.

Though she suspected the female didn't really require that information. Or appeared bothered by the way he'd spoken before she could even ask.

Was that common? It wasn't quite polite, but it wasn't rude, either.

"Follow me, please," the woman replied with a couple of menus in her hand.

He gestured for Odessa to go first. Right. That was the gentlemanly thing to do. She really had to pay attention to his actions and words. Despite his statement last night, both mattered, especially with relationships. Offering a slight grin, Odessa strode in front of him and trailed behind the female. She glanced around, drinking it all in, as the hostess led them to a table.

They passed a bar and rounded a corner, walking by two tall, deep-blue columns. Both of them were lit up. And looked beautiful. The woman passed by a couple of empty tables and stopped in front of a two-top. "Here we are," she stated as she set the menus down.

"Thank you," Odessa responded. She swept a hand beneath her black pencil skirt as she slipped into the booth side of the table.

"Yes, thank you," Austin echoed as he sat in his chair. "This place has excellent food." He cracked a smile at Odessa.

"Oh? So, you've tried it before?" It made sense he'd take her somewhere that he knew tasted good. At least for a first date. The same had happened when she first started dating Hamilton. It had taken months before they tried some place new.

"I've brought potential clients here. It comes highly recommended by my colleagues."

"What do you do?" A simple question. One of those typical get-to-know-you questions. She opened the menu and eyed the different options. Italian. Not something she expected from a place called Jupiter.

"I'm a lawyer." He chuckled. "I know I don't quite look the part, right?"

His response had to be because of the look on her face. She'd tried to keep control of it, but that didn't always work out. "Well, you fit the profile. The expensive suit is typically a giveaway for something more elite. Like a lawyer, high-end real estate agent, doctor, or a stockbroker."

"Don't think I've ever been compared to a real estate agent. That's new."

"I'm honest." The other three seemed more likely than a lawyer. His need to always be polite. Lawyers were renowned for their ability to lie. And he seemed to pride himself on being truthful.

"What about you? What kind of work do you do?"

"I'm a conservator at The Morck Library." She suspected she already knew the next question that would follow. Though his cocked eyebrow posed it without the words. Odessa let out a soft laugh. "I'm responsible for the repair and preservation of ancient texts there."

"Was my confusion that obvious?"

"Most people don't know exactly what we do." It didn't affect how much she loved her job. She flicked her gaze back to the menu. Three to four courses. Her gaze lifted as their server approached their table.

"Good evening. Welcome to Jupiter. My name is Matt and I'll be taking care of you this evening. Can I start you off with something to drink? Perhaps a glass of wine."

Normally, she didn't drink much. But given how things had gone over the last few days, a glass of wine sounded like heaven. And they had great options. "Yes, I think I'll take a glass of the Palazzotto. And a glass of water, please."

"Excellent choice, ma'am. And you, sir?"

"A glass of the Cirelli and water, as well."

"Of course. Have either of you decided on your first course? If not, I'll get your drinks."

Odessa glanced at Austin. "I'm ready, if you are." She spoke Italian, so it didn't take her long to figure out the various offerings. And it wasn't a big menu.

"Yes."

Well, that was good. Conversation had a tendency to distract people sometimes. Not that they'd spoken of anything all that important. "I'll start with the Bruschetta Di Granchio E Puntarelle."

"And I'll go with the Beef Sott'Olio," Austin tacked on.

Their server nodded to them both and left their table. That gave them at least a few minutes to talk before he returned. She flicked her gaze from the menu. "You seem surprised I chose so quickly."

"Most people ask questions about the different options. I know there's not a lot, but some words are confusing. And their descriptions aren't entirely helpful."

"Oh." Her cheeks heated a touch. "I speak Italian. That's why it's so easy for me. Wasn't sure if the server did, otherwise I would've ordered using it." Though she might've stumbled over a few words. She hadn't used it in several months. Perhaps she should brush up on it.

His eyes widened. "Wow. I didn't see that coming." Austin nodded appreciatively at her. "Do you speak other languages?"

"Read mostly, but yes, I do. Ancient Greek, Latin, and Sanskrit fluently. They help with my work." Any conservator worth their gumption learned old languages. Or even dead ones. Just depended on how far one went with their career. She had a great support system as she got her degrees.

"I guess that goes with the territory."

"Pretty much." *Oh, please don't let this be one of those dates where we run out of things to talk about quickly.* She'd had one or two in the past. Before her first date with Hamilton. Everything between them flowed so naturally. Maybe it was her. Maybe she just didn't make this easy for Austin.

"Well, that's kind of interesting. I bet you've seen a lot of things with your job. A lot of history."

"I do, but that's what I love about it. It's like I'm constantly watching our history unfold every day and how it shaped our world." Not to mention how it seemed they repeated some of those same mistakes. "Is that why you became a lawyer? Is it something you're passionate about?"

"It's actually a family legacy. Something passed down through the men in my family. So, it was expected."

"Wow. That seems like a lot to live up to." Her gaze shifted to their server as he returned with their drinks. She held her menu back as he set the wine glasses and glasses of water on the table.

"Are you ready to order?"

"Could you give us a few minutes?" Odessa asked. While she'd mostly figured out what she wanted to eat, they had a rapport going. Dinner could wait a second.

"Of course." He dipped his chin to the two of them and walked away from the table.

"I hope that was okay," she said to Austin.

"It's fine. I don't mind."

That was good to know. Since they had their wine, maybe they could do something that would establish a pleasant setting for their meal. She lifted her glass of wine. "A toast to a wonderful evening of companionship."

Austin picked up his glass and clinked hers. "To a wonderful evening."

As Odessa took a sip of wine, she watched as another couple got sat at the table opposite them. Odessa slowly lowered her glass as she caught sight of a face on the other side of the window behind the couple. It wasn't possible. She had to be seeing things. Had she thought about him so much to have literally compelled an image of him to her mind? That she'd see his chiseled face in something as simple as a window.

It had to be her imagination. She blinked. Nothing appeared behind the couple. It was nothing more than a clean window. Austin gripped her hand. "Hey. Odessa. Are you alright?"

She shook off whatever she thought she'd seen. It was all in her head. Whatever happened, it really seemed like she'd lost it. But now wasn't the time to discuss it, especially with someone she'd only just met. "Um, yeah." Her gaze flicked from him to the glass she'd actually dropped. Damn it.

"No worries, ma'am. Accidents happen," their server said.

Shit. When had he gotten there? "I'm so sorry." She'd had an episode that she couldn't explain. An apology was the only thing she could offer.

"It's alright." The server got the last of the spilled wine cleaned up and removed the empty glass. "I'll return with another one shortly."

"Thank you," Austin said. Once the server disappeared, he turned his attention to her. "Are you certain you're alright, Odessa? If something happened, you can tell me."

He was so sweet at the moment. While she refused to go into details, maybe she could give him something. Strange things had occurred yesterday morning. Maybe that was to blame. "I just thought I saw something. Guess my nerves got the best of me."

"We can go if you want. Go out another night?"

"No. I wouldn't have said yes if I didn't want to be here. And I refuse to let what happened take over my life." She didn't know what she'd seen, but it was gone now. Maybe it was something she could deal with later. Eventually, she'd have to take care of it. This wouldn't be her life. The ghost of her late-fiancé wouldn't chase her.

"Alright. Just so you know, I'll understand if you decide you want to leave."

"Thank you. I appreciate that." And she meant that. Now, they could enjoy the rest of their date without issue.

Hamilton slithered further into the shadows of a corner in Odessa's living room. Theoretically, he shouldn't have been able to get into her apartment without her permission. It seemed his sire had given him some inaccurate information. He'd slipped in easily through the window in her bedroom. And now he stood there invisibly, waiting for her to return from her date. Not that he should be, but he couldn't help himself.

Just like he hadn't stopped himself from peering at her through the window at the restaurant. He'd disappeared after she dropped her wine glass. Something that shouldn't have happened. But he'd gotten sloppy. He'd never done that before. Not even when they dated.

His ears perked at the sound of footsteps approaching the door. He listened to the ongoings in the outer hallway. While some part of him wanted her to move on and be happy, another couldn't stand the thought of truly losing her.

"Good night, Austin. I had a great time." Odessa said. "I look forward to doing it again."

"Me, too. Have a good night, Odessa."

The door to her apartment opened. Odessa locked her front door and slipped her heels off. Her kitten meowed, jumped down from the couch, and ran over to where she stood. She grinned at him. "It went okay. Though it might've been better if I hadn't imagined seeing my late fiancé."

God, what was wrong with him? This was complete and utter torture. Not just for him, but for her, too. He should leave. Walk around the couch and go out the same way that he'd come in.

But he couldn't do that. He needed to see her too badly. This was the closest he'd been to her in over a year. Even seeing her now stilled his heart. She was just as beautiful as the first time he saw her all those years ago.

Hamilton pushed the store's door open. He peered over his shoulder at his friend as they exited and plowed right into another person. "Oh, God. I'm so…" his words trailed off as his gaze shifted to the blonde-haired female right in front of him.

She narrowed her eyes at him, swept a strand of her golden locks behind her ear, and folded her arms across her chest. "Do you watch where you're going?"

Feisty. He liked it. Her beauty certainly drew him in, but her attitude reached down and grabbed him by the soul. There was just something about her. He stepped aside, holding the door open for her. "My apologies, Miss. I think I was just in too much of a hurry."

"Nothing of value in life is worth rushing toward." She smirked.

The dark-haired female behind her snickered. "If you plan to give him life lessons, Dess, I'm going to head inside."

"Go for it, Luce. I'll be along shortly."

He watched as her friend passed by him and disappeared inside. Since she, apparently, planned to scold him a bit more, it seemed pointless to keep the door open. He let it close after her friend. "Why don't you get the car?" Hamilton suggested to his best friend.

His companion shook his head and laughed. "Sure. Just don't take forever."

"Of course not." He just couldn't walk away until he got her phone number.

Or she agreed to see him again. Both were acceptable. "You're right. Good things come to those who wait… Dess? Is that right?"

"Odessa. Only my friends have the privilege of calling me Dess. Mr. Rude, I suggest you learn not to rush everywhere. It'll save you moments in the long run."

Wow. A beautiful name to go with a beautiful woman. "Hamilton, Miss Odessa. If you're going to talk some sense into me, then it would be best that you have my name."

"I suppose, but I don't really need to know your name. If I wanted it, I would've asked." With a smirk, she side-stepped him and went for the door.

"Ouch. You don't pull punches, do you?" Damn, this chick really had something about her. And with how she walked around him, getting to know her better might not be possible. But he refused to give up.

"I just call it like I see it." Odessa half-shrugged and entered the shop.

It had taken him two weeks before he ran into her again at that same store. Their second encounter went a little like their first, except he'd actually gotten her phone number that time. God, he missed her. This last year without her had been far too much to deal with. As much as he should have, he couldn't leave. Not yet. Hamilton stood in the corner and watched her.

She scooped the kitten up into her arms and sat on the sofa. "I'd like to think that I'm past his death. What if I'm not?"

The black furball purred and snuggled against her.

Some part of his heart swelled, but the other ached. She deserved better than this. He couldn't be selfish, no matter how much he wanted to be. It was bad enough she'd unintentionally gotten pulled into his world. Anything beyond what had already happened would be on his hands. He needed to let her go. Protect her from afar. Hamilton dropped his gaze to the hardwood floor. If he had any sense, he'd leave, but no matter how much he tried, his feet refused to budge.

"Is that your way of saying you agree?" She snickered. "That's it, isn't it? It's why I still think about him." Biting her bottom lip, she flicked her gaze toward the hallway. Odessa set the kitten down on the couch cushion to her right and stood. "Just stay put." She let out a small chuckle as he jumped down and trailed behind her.

This had certainly taken an interesting turn. He hadn't expected to hear or see any of this when he'd snuck into her apartment. Hamilton stepped out of the corner, but maintained his invisibility. It didn't seem wise to reveal himself to her. The last thing he wanted was to cause her any harm. He strolled around the couch until he could see what she did. Odessa opened the hall closet, flipped on the light, and retrieved a box from the top shelf.

What could be inside the box? Hamilton glanced around the living room, scanning the pictures scattered about. Most of them were of Odessa and her family, including the one she had of her mother and her as a child. A few were of Odessa and her best friend. The one thing missing… all the photographs they'd taken over their years together. His gaze snapped back to the box. Had she packed them away?

"I know this is probably insane," she said as she glanced down at the black furball. "But I can't stop myself. He was the love of my life." She shut the door and took the box into the living room, bypassing the television. Reclaiming her seat on the couch, she set the box down beside her and the kitten jumped up onto the cushion next to her. "Now's the time to stop me."

The kitten's only response was to rub up against her leg, climb into her lap, and curl up. Hamilton strode behind the couch and stopped just to the side of it. The kitten's head perked up, and it meowed. Shit. Had he dropped his invisibility? No. Odessa glanced in his direction, but shook her head. She didn't see him, though it appeared the black furball could. Interesting. He should step back. He shouldn't be this close, but he couldn't help himself. His heart raced and his palms got clammy. Not that he'd do anything about it. Other than stand here and watch.

"Guess that answers that." Odessa reached over, popped a couple of flaps up, and pulled out one of the photo albums.

Holy shit. He recognized that yellow pearled color. It wasn't something he'd easily forget. Did she know which album she held in her hands? Dumb question. No way was it something Odessa would've forgotten.

It was from their engagement.

She cracked it open. The corners of her mouth lifted into a smile. "Oh, God," she muttered. Tears pricked the corners of her eyes.

Everything he'd planned had one goal—take her breath away. Hamilton had gone above and beyond anything romantic he'd ever done for her. It had taken him months to organize it all, but in the end, it had been worth it.

He'd taken her on her first hot-air balloon ride. Before going on the ride, they'd gotten to watch them fill the balloons, and then witnessed the most beautiful sunrise together. The sun had crested into so many exquisite hues of purple, orange, and yellow. To top it off, they'd traveled across the Santa Barbara sky, floating over the surrounding vineyards and gorgeous ranches. Wine country had never looked more stunning. The proposal came when they'd landed. After they'd stepped off, he got down on one knee and popped the question.

The champagne flowed with her resounding yes. They loved one another so much. She stroked a finger across their engagement photograph, caressing his cheek. "I miss you so much." Odessa sighed as she curled her fingers against the page of photos and wiped the tears from her face.

He missed her, too. In ways he hadn't ever imagined possible, especially with how things had so abruptly ended. Their last day together popped into his mind. Their last argument. A culmination of all the secrets he'd kept from her.

"You're leaving again?" Odessa demanded.

"I'm sorry, Dess, but I have to go. This is important." How could he tell her the truth? Something he'd wanted to do for a long time now. Although his mother encouraged it, his uncle continued to remind him why he couldn't. That if she knew, it would endanger her life. While that was something he feared, he worried more that she'd lose control of her mind. Odessa had fought so hard not to follow her mother's path of insanity. The truth would only make

it that much harder, especially when his world was so much darker than he'd ever allowed her to believe.

"If it's so important, then why can't you tell me what commands so much of your attention?"

Hamilton gently gripped her arms. He desperately needed her to listen and trust him. "Please, believe me, Dess. If I could tell you, I would, but your safety is far too important to me."

Odessa shrugged his hold off of her body. "My safety." She scoffed. "Is that why you're digging into grimoires? Because I thought we were over this whole witch nonsense?" Shaking her head, she folded her arms across her chest. "Just go. Because nothing you say is something I can believe."

"Dess…" his words trailed off. Would she believe him if he told her the truth? That he and his uncle were going to hunt a witch tormenting the town. That things that went bump in the night were more than just a myth. Or would she think him insane?

"Just go!" she screamed.

"Fine." He grabbed his bag and jerked it over his shoulder. Maybe it was time he told her the truth. He'd kept this a secret from her long enough. And he didn't want to marry her with this still between them. After he got back, he'd be honest with her about all he'd hidden over the years. It was time. And a risk he had to take. No matter the consequences. "We'll talk when I get home."

Not that they'd ever had that conversation. He never came home. At least, not in the way they expected. Against his better judgment and his sire's warnings, he'd visited Odessa in their home twice while she slept. Almost like he did now, except she was awake. She flipped to the next page in the album. More tears trickled down her cheeks as she rubbed at her chest. God, he couldn't stand seeing her like this.

Stepping around the couch, he kneeled down and became visible to her. "Please, don't cry."

"Oh, God. I did it again." With a shake of her head, she scrubbed her face. "I can't keep doing this."

"Do what?" he asked. Though he suspected she believed that she'd imagined him there.

"Conjured you in my mind. I'm trying so hard to move forward. This is supposed to be a fresh start."

Despite how much he wanted to reach out and comfort her, he couldn't. He only had his words. They'd have to be enough. Otherwise, she'd know something was off. "It's okay to think about me. We spent years together and meant a lot to one another. That doesn't mean you haven't moved on. Remember how you used to think about your mom? Talking to her helped you through a lot of stressful times. You told me that. Maybe this is just a moment where you need me."

"Maybe." Odessa half-nodded and brushed the rest of the tears from her face.

Her response didn't instill much in the way of confidence in him. Had he screwed up somehow? No. Her features softened a bit. Now, he just had to convince her that this was all in her head. Hamilton rose to his feet, straightening to his full height. "I'm always here for you, Dess. I'll never stop watching over you."

"I know." She shut the photo album. "But I need to learn how to handle things without you. You're not actually here. Just a memory."

Her reply should've thrilled him. It was exactly what he hoped to accomplish. That didn't make it hurt any less. He wanted her to be happy. It was all he'd ever wanted. But that didn't change how much he missed her. Especially seeing her over these last few days. Not that it would stop him from watching over her. He could face the heartache if it meant keeping her safe. That was his burden to bear. "Then you know what you need to do."

"Yes, I do, but that doesn't make it easy."

"It's okay, Dess. Just close your eyes and think about the life you have ahead of you. Your dreams. Your future. The rest will take care of itself." It seemed the best way to go invisible. Though he could've handled things another way, that route seemed a bit more invasive.

Odessa dipped her chin in acknowledgment, shut her eyes, and stroked her fingers through her kitten's fur. She inhaled and exhaled a couple of deep breaths.

He wished they could have more time together, but he'd already taken enough of a risk. Hamilton went invisible, strode toward the hallway, and glanced back over his shoulder one last time. As much as he wanted to wait until she opened her eyes, he couldn't. "I love you, Odessa," he whispered and disappeared down the hall, leaving the same way he'd entered.

five

WITH HIS CLOTHES CHANGED, HAMILTON descended the staircase and headed toward the dining room. Although he'd spent a few minutes talking to Odessa last night, it hadn't been nearly enough. Something he couldn't mention to his sire. His desire to spend more time with her would only get her hurt. He had to be careful and train with his new powers the way he should've months ago.

"Good morning," he said to his sire as he entered the dining room. He strode over to the table and sat in the chair to Theo's right. It was just the two of them, though the table could certainly accommodate several more people.

"Good morning," Theo replied as he shook out the newspaper. "You came home earlier than I expected last night. Have you tired of your librarian already?"

"She went on a date." He flicked his gaze briefly to his sire as one maid served his breakfast. "Don't worry. I left the human intact," he lied, as if it was second nature. Something he'd done far too many times over the course of his life, but Theo had to believe him.

"I'm glad to hear that."

"Here, I thought you'd chastise me." It seemed to be what Theo did the most. Though he never really listened. Well, he heard it. He just didn't pay it any attention.

"Why would I do that when you finally showed some restraint?" Theo took a sip from his coffee mug and turned the page of the newspaper.

The doorbell rang.

His sire didn't react at all. They didn't get visitors, especially during the day. The shutters were closed, so no sunlight got into the house, except some would shine into the foyer as the butler opened the front door. Maybe it shouldn't bother him. It could be nothing of importance. Hamilton added a couple of sugar cubes to his coffee and stirred it. "It wasn't without great effort." Which was true; though it didn't apply to seeing her, it did to his yearning to touch her.

"It wouldn't be restraint if it was easy."

Yeah, sure. Sometimes, conversing with his sire drove him crazy. "What kind of training are we working on?" He got into his breakfast. Something that hadn't changed even after Theo had turned him. He hadn't expected to eat food, but it was one of those strange occurrences that applied to him and Theo. Perhaps that was why.

"We'll be downstairs. I've set the training room up for us. We'll use your new speed and strength. Amongst other things."

He hadn't ever seen the training room. It had to be big if he'd have to use his speed. Probably should've seen it before now, but it hadn't been important. Something he'd have to change. The front door shut. "Whatever you show me, I'll work on regularly."

"Perhaps your librarian should've arrived in town sooner. Her presence has done wonders for your determination."

"Can we not discuss Odessa?" While she'd never leave his mind, he didn't want to talk about her with his sire.

"Of course." Theo lifted his gaze as the butler approached with a sealed envelope. "Thank you, Grayson."

"You're welcome, sir." The butler bowed and disappeared from the room.

"What's that?" As he took another bite, he gestured to the white paper. He couldn't make out much other than a red-wax seal. Was it something important? Or just day-to-day stuff he didn't handle?

His sire set the newspaper aside, flicked his eyes to Hamilton, and let out a small sigh. "Something from the council." Using a knife, he sliced open the envelope and removed a piece of parchment. With a growl, he slammed it down on the table. "I told you that your antics would lead to this."

"What?" Hamilton picked up the piece of paper and read over it. Son of a bitch. He tossed his fork down and dragged a hand down his face. "A summons? Before the council? Seriously?"

"I told you not to draw attention to yourself. Do you understand how bad this could get?"

"There's no way they could know about my past or anything about Odessa." He crossed his arms. "Any way we can just ignore this?"

"No. You've been summoned. We must go." Theo rose to his feet. "We'll train as scheduled. And handle the council… as diplomatically as possible. Understood?"

Which meant he wouldn't speak or utter a single word. Simple enough. As he'd never met the council, it might be best he actually listened for once. "Yes, sir."

"Good. Now, finish up. Training begins in thirty minutes."

Odessa stared at the portrait of Hamilton Morck. How many photo albums had she gone through last night after she'd banished the ghost of Hamilton from her mind? Too many to count. The more she eyed the different photographs and the longer she stared at this painting, the more certain she was they were the same person. But how was that possible? Looking exactly the same didn't make them the same person. She'd seen her late fiancé's dead body. She'd gone with Gladys to identify it.

No. All of this was just in her head. Her heart ached still from the loss that her imagination went beyond the wildest direction possible. A way to keep him alive in more than just her mind. She sighed heavily. Standing here when she was supposed to be working was wrong. There were too many people around the library.

"He's hot, isn't he? Not that I think that portrait does him justice," one of her colleagues stated.

Odessa cocked an eyebrow at Morgan. "I didn't think anyone had met him." That's what Laura had told her. Had the female lied? Or was it what the female believed?

"No one has met him directly. I've only seen him once in passing. But the last conservator set up an e-mail for communication. Didn't Laura tell you about that?"

"No, she didn't." An e-mail, huh? She lifted her eyes back to the portrait. As uncanny as their similarities were, no way could she send an e-mail to him. But what if she did? Maybe then she could discern something about this guy. That sounded like a decent idea. "Can you show me?"

"Of course." Morgan glanced at her gold watch. "I've got time now if you do."

"Absolutely." It wasn't like this was a crazy idea. And she had a reason to e-mail this Hamilton person. A small introduction as the new conservator. Though she could pose a few questions, too. The two of them started toward the elevator.

"I'm surprised she didn't teach you about it."

"Well, I wanted to dive right into things. And honestly, that tour got long and boring." Not that she expected much differently. They usually filled the first few days of any new job with drivel. She could've dealt without most of it. Especially as the important information got left out.

"I can understand that." Morgan depressed the elevator button.

She glimpsed the female out of the corner of her eye. Something Morgan said earlier nagged at her in the back of her mind. Odessa shoved her hands in her skirt pockets. "When did you cross paths with Mr. Morck?"

"A few months back. He came in one night just as I was leaving. I think he headed downstairs, but I can't say for sure."

It made sense that he had a lot to do with the collection on the lower floors. Could he have left those books out the other night? Did he know better? If he spent the time to invest in them, she supposed so, but that wasn't always the case. The elevator door opened and she and Morgan climbed into it. "Do you know if that's common?"

Morgan pushed the button for one floor down. "No idea. Not that it would surprise me. Our owners have always come and gone as they pleased."

"Really? At all times of day?" It would explain the noises she thought she'd heard the other night. Even if she couldn't figure out why Laura hadn't heard anything. Or her mind just played tricks on her.

"Oh, yeah. Why not? They have keys and know all the alarm codes." Morgan shrugged as the elevator door opened.

The two of them exited and hooked a right, heading toward the administrative office. She'd gone in there only once since she started, but hadn't paid much attention to everything in there. Something else about this place bothered her a little. She needed to know something. "Is there a book here that talks about the history of this library?"

"Somewhere, but I'm uncertain where. Though I have knowledge about this place. What would you like to know?"

Well, she had several questions. Where did she start? It might be best that she avoided some of her stranger questions. "When was this place established? Was it always named *The Morck Library*?"

"Yes. The Morck family has owned it since 1792, but Hamilton Morck, he didn't come into the picture until a year ago. That's when things got started with the preservation room. I was a bit surprised how quickly it all came together."

Yeah, that didn't sound fishy at all. While she had several other questions, it was best that she do her own research. Especially with the absurdity of what all ran through her mind. The two of them stopped at the administrative office. She had an e-mail to send.

Hamilton eyed the mansion as they approached. It was unlike anything he'd ever seen before. At least three, maybe four, stories high. Built entirely of stone. It had to be a few centuries old. Not that he could say for sure. Nor did he really care. The only thing on his mind, aside from this meeting, was the e-mail he'd received from Odessa. His heart had fluttered earlier at the sight. Even though it had everything to do with work, he still couldn't get the words out of his head.

Good afternoon Mr. Morck,

My name is Odessa Black. I'm your new conservator. I wanted to introduce myself and reach out regarding a few concerns. While we can resolve some via e-mail, if it suits you, I'd like to schedule a time when we can sit down together and discuss the future of the lower levels.

The display cases in the preservation room have some of the most ancient tomes I've ever seen. However, these cases have no lock. I'd recommend changing this, as they should be well-protected against any type of theft. I also noticed the entry code is rather easy to discern. It's my belief we should change this to something more complex. It also might be beneficial to have the hand-washing stations prepped to prevent any leakage. Although I've mentioned these concerns to you, I'll also make these some suggestions to the library manager.

I'd appreciate your thoughts on my recommendations. I was also told the previous conservator often selected books that might work well with the current collection. Do you know if she

left a list of what she was seeking prior to her departure?

Thank you for your time. I look forward to hearing from you soon.

Sincerely,

Odessa Black

Despite the importance of this summons, he'd taken some time to craft a response. As much as he desired to meet with her, he couldn't do that. Not as Hamilton Morck. Too many questions would follow, provided she didn't pass out at the sight of him. He dragged a hand down his face as the town car came to a stop. Great. This wasn't something he looked forward to, but he couldn't stop it either. Hamilton eyed his sire out of his periphery. "Are you certain we must attend to this?"

"There is no choice. I told you this earlier. We cannot ignore a summons. Let us just pray they don't know anything."

Yeah, he refused to touch that. He learned a long time ago that it was pointless to pray about things. God never responded. And even if the guy did for hunters, He definitely wouldn't do it for vampires. Their species were supposed to be the epitome of evil. Not that he felt that way. Then again, he was an anomaly. "Fine," he grumbled. His door opened. Hamilton climbed out of the car and tugged on the hem of his jacket's sleeves. They just needed to get this over with.

His sire approached him from the back of the car and joined him. "Shall we?" Theo nodded his head at the front door.

"Lead the way." Not like they had any other choice. The male had pointed that out multiple times already. At least their training session from this morning had taken off some of the edge. He might actually get through this without saying something stupid, especially since he didn't know how to act around the different clans.

Theo strode to the heavy wooden door. It looked old and dark, but matched what he'd seen of the house. He lifted the knocker, rapped twice on the door, and clasped his hands at the small of his back.

A few moments later, the door opened and an older gentleman in black livery greeted them. "Good evening, Lord Morck. Please, come in." He stepped aside, giving them passage.

Hamilton trailed behind his sire as he took in his surroundings. Everything about this place screamed *old*, from the paintings hanging on the walls to the statues lining the hallway. Even the gilded banister he could see from the hall. Not that it applied to everything. Like the marble floor. The furniture looked like a mix between the two. Some pieces appeared more traditional from the early 1800s or earlier, while others seemed closer to the 21st century.

It was kind of strange to see such a combination. Maybe they'd replaced pieces over the years and went with something current. Some things were harder to come by these days. Though he suspected if they took the time, they could find the right pieces. Did this mean the heads of each clan didn't agree on something as simple as décor? If that was the case, what did that mean for him?

He followed Theo into a massive study. Seven chairs sat on an elevated platform against one wall while floor-to-ceiling bookcases lined the others. The number of books this place contained nearly matched the collection at the library. At least it appeared close to the same number, if not more. Given the size of the manor, this room was likely only one of a few filled with books. He'd love to explore the house more, though they probably wouldn't let him.

Six males occupied the chairs. One seat remained empty. They hadn't arrived early. Theo had ensured they'd gotten here right on time. The male prided himself on punctuality.

Theo stopped several feet in front of the platform and bowed his head to those gathered. "My Lords," he said. "I present a recent addition to my family, Hamilton Morck."

"The pleasure is mine," he stated as he bowed, just as his sire had instructed him. Protocol dictated he give the heads of the clans his respect, even if he didn't feel they deserved it. What information his sire had given him wasn't nearly enough to truly know any of them, so he couldn't really make that judgment call.

"Of that, I'm certain," the middle clan head replied. His dark gaze shifted to Theo. "Perhaps, Lord Morck, you'd like to give some introductions before we get down to business. Or have you already handled that?"

"I took care of it this morning, Sir Isaac," his sire replied.

Yep, he'd gotten an earful of things to remember. All so he could recognize the males sitting on their thrones, according to Theo. Along with how to act and address the clan heads. The only one he didn't see among their leaders was Sebastian McCrae. From what Theo had told him, that was the head of their clan. At least he assumed that was the missing person. He didn't know what the guy looked like. Neither had Theo.

"Excellent." Sir Isaac steepled his fingers together in his lap. "Then let us begin." A faint smile flickered across the male's face. "Hamilton Morck, you stand here today accused of attacking another vampire, which is against our laws. How do you plead?"

Attempting to keep his face neutral, he glanced at his sire out of his periphery. He had fought against another vampire, something he'd explained to Theo the other night. But the guy hadn't said one word about it being against the rules. Instead, he'd only chastised him, which seemed customary for them. While some part insisted on lying, it wouldn't be wise. Though he was well-trained against mental attacks, at least one vampire on the council could read minds. "I fought with another vampire; however, it wasn't without cause."

"Cause does not constitute a valid excuse to break one of our sacred laws," Sir Isaac commented.

"Let us not be so quick to judge," the dark-haired male at the end tacked on. "I would like to hear his reason. Please proceed." He gestured his hand with a slight flourish at Hamilton.

Things got tricky here. He had to tell the truth without admitting too much. Hamilton nodded his head. "I was following a new employee home, watching over her from the rooftops. That was when I noticed another trailed after her. It wasn't until I attacked that I even realized they were a vampire."

"This… employee," Isaac uttered with disdain, "is a human, correct?"

"Yes," Hamilton replied. It seemed unwise to add anything else. He didn't want any of them to discover how much Odessa meant to him.

"Then why see her home? Humans are nothing more than food. Unless this is a service you provide to all of your employees?" the male posed.

Yeah, the ideation he expected. These vampires had no respect for humans. Not that it should surprise him. They'd all been born vampires and likely had little interaction with humans. Still, he had a simple answer. "As most of them work during the day, it's unnecessary. Though, after what happened to my last conservator, I believe in protecting this one."

Silence stretched amongst the clan leaders. None of them could dismiss him so easily after that. A vampire had killed the female who'd helped him establish the lower level of the library. Every single one of them knew it. Not that anything had ever happened to the responsible party.

A blond male with bright-green eyes who sat two seats down from Isaac tilted his head. He tapped his chin as he scrutinized Hamilton. "While there is truth to your words, there is something you're not sharing about this female. Something… special about her. She means something to you. Beyond her status in your establishment."

Shit. Theo had told him most of the council members had other abilities outside the normal. Though he'd failed to mention what each could do. Obviously, he hadn't hidden things as much as he'd hoped. Hamilton ground his jaw and swallowed saliva to wet his parched throat. He couldn't object or deny the truth.

"I will take your abject silence as confirmation. Who is this female? How is she important to you?" Isaac asked.

Regardless of how much he didn't want to answer, he had no choice. "She is someone from my former life."

"I'm certain my question was quite clear. Who is she?"

Hadn't he given them enough? Wasn't the point of this inquisition about his attack on another vampire? How had it gotten to this? And how did he keep *her* from further involvement? He glanced at Theo. There had to be something he could say. Anything. But what? Hamilton clenched his fingers together tightly, opened his mouth, and snapped it shut. No matter how hard he tried, no words came forth.

"That is quite alright. I see the answer we seek," the blond uttered. He glanced at the other council members. "She was his fiancée. The love of his life. I believe we know how to handle this situation."

"You're right," Isaac responded. "Hamilton Morck, we find you guilty as charged. For your punishment, you have two options. One, turn this woman or two, kill her. We will expect your answer in two nights. You're both dismissed."

"What?" Hamilton snapped. "No! You can't do this. Odessa has nothing to do with our world." How could they make such an irrational decision? All because he'd gotten his ass kicked by another vampire. It didn't matter that he'd started it to protect her. This was completely insane.

"We've made our decision." Isaac glared at Hamilton. "Be grateful we gave you a choice."

"Thank you, my lords. We will return as requested," Theo interjected, before Hamilton could say anything else.

His sire grabbed his arm and ushered him out of the large room. The male practically dragged him down the hall and forced him to leave the manor. "We have to do something," he growled at Theo. "I'm not turning or killing her."

"We will," his sire replied in a hushed tone. "But we need to go now lest you make things worse."

"Fine! Just know where I stand." Because neither choice they gave was an option. He'd kill every clan leader before he let anyone harm Odessa.

six

ODESSA STIRRED AWAKE AND ROLLED over onto her side. She slowly opened her eyes, adjusting to the moonlight streaming through the sheer curtains of her bedroom window. It lit her room up beautifully. Her gaze shifted to the corner. "Hamilton," she uttered in a sleepy voice. Whatever had caused her to conjure him more over the last few days, she didn't care. Not right now.

"Hi, Dess." He cracked a soft smile at her as he approached her bedside.

"I was dreaming about you." While she couldn't explain why, she scooched over to make room for him. It made no sense. He had no corporeal form. His only existence was in her head.

"Oh? Anything specific?"

"Our disastrous first date." Since she'd looked through their engagement album last night, so much of their relationship played in her mind on an endless loop. All nine years of it. Both the bad and the good.

Chuckling, he sat on the edge of the bed. "I don't recall it being so awful. Maybe a bit on the messy side, but that just made it even more memorable."

"Messy, huh?" Odessa smirked. "I threw up all over your shoes and you had to take me to the emergency room. That sounds way more than just *messy.*" None of that included how her face had swollen from an unknown seafood allergy. Though she'd agree with the latter part. It made it a date to remember.

"But think about how much we learned about each other that night. We covered more than most people do in the first few weeks of a new relationship."

That they did. With as much as it had taken him to convince her to give him her phone number, that night she realized it was the best decision she'd ever made. He'd shown her exactly what kind of male he was.

The door to her hospital room cracked open, and Hamilton poked his head around the corner. "Is it okay to come in?"

Odessa scrunched her eyebrows. "Um, sure. I, um, I'm surprised you're still here." For sure, she'd thought he'd left hours ago. They'd been there long enough. It's why she'd told the nurse to call her brother. Plus, she hadn't wanted her father to fret. Not to mention, he might try to blame her date for something that wasn't his fault.

"Of course, I am. I wanted to make sure you were okay." He slipped into her room, gently shut the door, and gestured to the chair beside the bed. "May I?"

"Sure." Most guys she'd met wouldn't have stuck around. Not all of them would've even taken her to the emergency room after she'd thrown up. At least the ones she'd gone out with. Though this kind of thing didn't happen often. It wasn't like she could judge Hamilton based on the actions of someone that she'd previously dated.

Hamilton sat in the chair and grasped her hand within his own. The warmth of his palm sent a shiver down her spine. "You look better."

"I feel better. Guess that's what happens when they pump you full of drugs." She let out a small laugh. That probably wasn't as funny as it sounded in her mind. Odessa shrugged. "I had an allergic reaction to the lobster." It would figure that her first time trying something and she got sick. "That's never happened before with seafood, but I've only ever had shrimp."

"I'm glad to hear it. You had me worried earlier."

The corner of her mouth lifted into a half-grin. "Are you always concerned about people you hardly know? Or are you just trying to make a better impression?" It seemed like a dumb question, though she'd intended it to be funny. They'd only met a few weeks ago. Although she'd thought he was cute the day they met, she'd also seen him as a bit of a goof. The way he held her hand and stroked his thumb across the top suggested otherwise.

"Hmm, that's a tough call. Maybe a bit of both. Though we both know your attraction to me was immediate." He chuckled.

"Oh my God, you are so full of yourself." Funny, charming, and caring. She couldn't have asked for better qualities in a male. It may only be their first date, but she could easily see building a life with him.

"Before or after, my brother broke up our little tête-à-tête." Odessa yawned. Whatever had caused her to wake no longer appeared to affect her. Or the memory had relaxed her in a way she hadn't expected. Either way, sleep called out to her.

"Get some rest, Dess. You look like you could use it."

"Yeah," she mumbled as she covered her mouth, stifling another yawn. If nothing else, at least she could go back to her dreams. Where all was right in the world. And they were together.

"Where are we?" Hamilton glanced from Theo to the high-rise the car stopped in front of. Had the male come up with some solution to the punishment the council posed to him last night? His sire had locked himself in his study before he'd gone to check on Odessa. It hadn't changed when he'd returned home afterward. Theo had been exactly where he'd left him.

"Hopefully, someone who can convince the council their decree is nothing short of insanity and goes against our code of ethics."

"You mean like the law I supposedly broke? Or is it just something that works when it favors the council?" Yeah, nothing had altered his opinion of them more than what they wanted. It didn't sound like a code existed at all. If it did, no way would they force him to turn or kill a human being.

Theo let out a heavy sigh. "Can we not get into this again?"

"Sure. Let's go meet this person." Provided they existed. The last twenty-four hours hadn't given him much hope or reason to trust his sire had his best interest at heart. Unfortunately, he didn't have anyone else to turn to regarding the situation. Except Odessa. And he was already walking a dangerous line, pretending to be the ghost she imagined in her mind. He couldn't put her any further at risk.

Hamilton didn't bother waiting for Grayson to open his door, as the male did for Theo. He just wanted to get this over with. His gaze lifted to the extremely tall building with so many windows it would be impossible to count. What would it take to clean all of that? "Lead the way," he mumbled to his sire as he trailed after him.

"It would do you well to be a bit more respectful." Theo strode forward and entered a building with a lot of gold inlays along the walls. None of which included the exquisite paintings that hung in various places.

This didn't look like any apartment building he'd ever visited. Then again, they were in Manhattan. Whoever they'd come to see had to be someone of importance. "Unlike you, I don't require the driver to do everything for me. I'm almost surprised Grayson doesn't burp you."

Theo narrowed his piercing, blue eyes at him as they stopped in front of an elevator. "Then perhaps it would do you well to remember your place. As Grayson does."

Did the guy really think that scared him? Maybe he didn't have a great hold of his vampiric abilities, but his hunter abilities hadn't gone anywhere. Hmm, something he'd never considered before. Continuing to hunt the undead as a vampire. It was a thought, but one he'd have to think about more. Right now, he couldn't afford to do anything stupid. "I know my place. That doesn't mean it's what you believe."

With a ding, the elevator doors opened. The two of them stepped on, and Theo depressed the button for the sixty-seventh floor. Hamilton raised an eyebrow. Were they seriously going to the very top of the building? At least his hoity-toity assumption seemed accurate. "This is going to be a long ride," he muttered as the doors shut.

"That means it will give you plenty of time to reconsider your manners. After all, our goal is to address your situation. Not see how you can make it worse."

That seemed an impossible task. Unless he offended the person, they headed to visit. Then he could end up dead. That might be far-fetched. And wouldn't that person then have to answer to the council? Hamilton frowned. "Who are we going to see, anyway? Please, don't give me some half-assed answer."

"Sebastian. The head of our clan. As he was notably absent from last night's proceedings, I believe it might be worth checking in with him."

Well, that certainly confirmed his suspicions. His sire had lied about knowing the male. Why? How did it help Theo? Hamilton shoved his hands into the front pockets of his tweed dress pants. "I take it that's not normal? For him to miss a council meeting like that."

"Correct. Especially with decisions regarding punishments. He's a bit more modern for his age, which offers a balance with the others."

"That sounds like a polite way of saying they're all stuck up." And in need of a good ass-kicking. Something he'd happily provide. Maybe after a little more training. It wasn't like he questioned how old a vampire was when he killed them as a hunter. As confident as he was in his abilities, the council might prove formidable. In more ways than one.

"I'm uncertain I would say that. Simply that… they are each unique in their own way."

Yeah, he maintained his last response. "Is it par for the course for the three that spoke to… handle a council meeting?" *Or take it over*, he thought to himself. It was pointless to voice the question aloud. His sire wouldn't actually answer it.

"Isaac, Ashton, and Devereaux don't often control the meetings, though I've always found them the most vocal. So, it's difficult to say if others might offer any insight or disagree with their decisions."

It might not make a difference if they sought any of those other males out. He pinched the bridge of his nose as the elevator slowed to a stop. It hadn't taken as long as he'd initially expected. No one had joined them on the elevator and it hadn't stopped once between the first floor and here. The doors opened, and he followed Theo out and to the left. Hamilton returned his hand to his pocket with a heavy sigh. "Maybe instead of trying to get another opinion, we should work on coming up with our own options. Like how to alter the patriarchal society that the council has created."

Theo clasped his hands at the small of his back and smirked. "You cannot expect to change centuries of rules overnight. If you do, then you're quite fooling yourself."

Although the guy had a point; it was a thought. But it would mean he'd have to interact with other vampires more. Socialize and all that crap. Definitely different from the lifestyle of a hunter. Of course, hunters were born into a family of them. Not turned into them. "You're right. That's more of a long-term solution. We need something more immediate."

"Which is exactly why we're seeking Sebastian's counsel."

"Are you positive he's the answer? I mean, no offense, but we haven't even got to his place yet and I'm already feeling like he might fall in line with the others." This building was no castle, but it looked just as fancy as what he'd seen last night. Hell, even similar to the mansion he lived in. And that wasn't some place he'd chosen for himself.

"Yes. Sebastian simply enjoys the view and prefers his privacy. Otherwise, I suspect he might live out by the beach as we do."

"If you say so." Not that Theo had convinced him. He'd believe it when their clan leader came up with another idea. One that excluded the options presented. Hamilton followed his sire around another corner and down the hall, all the way to the end. At least the apartment was in the back. That offered a small amount of comfort.

Theo lightly rapped his knuckles on the door. Silence stretched between them as they waited. No answer came, so Theo knocked a second time.

Something about the lack of response bothered him. Though he couldn't pinpoint what. Hamilton rubbed his eyes and dragged a hand down his face. "Please tell me we didn't come all this way, and you failed to ensure he was home."

"Actually, I didn't expect him to be, but that has little to do with why we're here."

That made no sense. They'd come here to talk to this guy, which meant he had to be present. Hamilton shook his head. "Are you planning for us to wait in the lobby? Or am I missing something?"

"I told you. Sebastian never misses a meeting. If he's not home or answering his phone, I'd like to ensure we haven't overlooked anything."

Right. Theo had sold him a bunch of bullshit. Was that why he'd dragged him along? A second pair of eyes and shit. Hamilton bit back a groan. God, he'd like to knock his sire on his ass. "How do you propose we get inside? Because that doesn't look like a lock I can pick."

"Must you always go to something so barbaric?" Theo reached into the inside pocket of his coat and produced a key.

Of course, the male had a key. Why hadn't he thought about that? Which meant Theo *really* knew Sebastian. How close were they? "Then let's get inside before anyone becomes nosey."

"I'm certain we don't have to worry about that."

He preferred they didn't chance it. Though, if experience had taught him anything, if he pushed too much more, then his sire would take his time. Hamilton kept his mouth shut. Instead, he folded his arms across his chest and lightly tapped the toe of his loafers against the carpeted floor. It likely annoyed Theo, but he didn't care. The guy got the point.

With a slight scoff, Theo unlocked the door, opened it, and slipped inside. Hamilton trailed behind him, quietly closing the door before anyone noticed. They stepped into a small foyer and his sire strode over to a keypad and inputted a code. The security alarm shouldn't surprise him. This foyer looked nothing like the one he'd grown accustomed to over the last year. Ahead to the right, he spotted the living room and dining area directly across from the kitchen. At least from what he could make out.

The apartment was eerily silent. And on the cold side. More so than he expected, even for this time of year. Not that it appeared any of the windows were open. This place simply looked…empty. It wasn't devoid of any furnishings, but it didn't seem lived in, either. The hairs on the back of his neck stood at attention. Hamilton strode forward and glanced around. "Do you feel that?"

"Yes. Something feels…off," Theo replied.

That sounded like a good way to describe it, but it went deeper than that. He couldn't quite explain the sensations coursing through his body. His stomach rolled and his chest tingled. "Maybe we should just leave," he suggested.

"No. We need to push through and search the apartment. Find something that may tell us what happened…or where he could be."

What exactly did his sire expect they'd find? The place emulated neatness and organization. Nothing appeared out of place. Or at least out of the ordinary. Biting back a heavy sigh, Hamilton gripped the back of his neck and strolled forward. Maybe he'd locate the answer to this gut feeling. It would make the trip worthwhile if that happened. "Then we should split up." He took a few steps, stopping at the edge of a hallway to the side of the kitchen. "I'll take the back half and you take the front." The quicker they got through this, the faster they got out of here.

"Agreed," Theo replied.

The two of them went off in two separate directions. His sire started toward the living room, while he headed down the hallway and briefly lingered at the corner. From where he stood, he noticed four bedrooms. Not that he could make out what each contained. With a shake of his head, Hamilton rounded the corner and made his way to the back of the apartment. It was as good a place to begin as any of the others.

He paused inside the doorway of the far bedroom. His gaze flicked from one wall to the next, each covered with floor-to-ceiling bookcases. Holy shit. The sheer number of books lining the shelves accelerated his heart rate. Sebastian's collection was impressive. It didn't just comprise fictional works of authors like Shakespeare and Poe, but it also contained a lot of old books. Most of which had no titles, at least nothing he could immediately discern.

Hamilton crossed the room and scanned a few of the unmarked works. He randomly selected one, removed it from the shelf, and flipped through a couple of pages. *Shapeshifters?* What would a vampire be doing with this? Especially one who headed a clan. How had this guy even come across something like this? He returned the book to its proper location and retrieved another.

In a matter of minutes, he found at least three other tomes that referenced shapeshifters and two that mentioned vampires. Only one of those made sense to him. Why research shapeshifters? Did it go beyond the whole 'mortal enemies' thing? Or was he over-analyzing it? None of it offered any insight into where Sebastian had gone. Hamilton shook his head and peered around the room. He strolled to a desk in the corner with a small lamp. As he switched the light on, he sat in the chair. His eyes widened at the book laying open before him.

What the fuck?

This tome had disappeared from his family's vault years ago. It couldn't be right. Except the pages regarding hunters, detailing information on their way of life stared him in the face. He remembered reading these pages as a child. How had Sebastian come into possession of this book? An answer he'd seek later. Hamilton shut the book, tucked it into the back of his pants, and hid it discreetly beneath his jacket.

Pushing the chair back a bit with his feet, he opened one drawer after another and scoured through collections of paper. They'd come to this apartment to find information that would help them locate Sebastian. That's what he intended to look for, no matter what else he found.

Regardless of how many drawers and papers he scoured through, all he discovered was a conglomeration of notes. None of which he understood. Either the male had come up with his own form of shorthand or it was in some foreign language he didn't know. One of those moments where he needed Odessa's brain. As an afterthought, he snapped a couple of quick photos of the papers with his cell phone. Not that he could show her any of it. Shaking his head, he shoved it all back into the drawer. Nothing in or on the desk aided in their endeavor. Hamilton stood, returned the chair to its rightful position, and left the study.

Across the hall was a bathroom. He poked his head in the doorway, turned on the light switch and glanced over it. Nothing of importance stood out to him. He flipped off the light and moved onto the next bedroom. The dresser and nightstand were completely empty. If the dust was anything to go by, no one had used it in quite some time.

Hamilton left the room, stepped into the hallway, and paused outside the third bedroom. He shoved his hands into the pockets of his slacks. "I don't know about you, but if I had to hazard a guess, I'd say Sebastian hasn't been home in weeks."

"I agree," Theo called out over his shoulder. "This is a spare, so its emptiness doesn't surprise me. I expected to at least find something in his bedroom. It proved just as empty as the rest of the apartment. Did you find anything in his study?"

"A bunch of notes that I couldn't read, but that's it." He refused to mention the tomes. His sire knew this place and, given the key and code, the guy had some kind of relationship with Sebastian. More than the male bothered to admit. Theo had likely spent time here in the past, but how much? Had he ever used Sebastian's study? Or seen any of the books in the male's possession? Questions he didn't think his sire would answer if asked.

"I'm not sure anyone would. Sebastian has his own shorthand. To my knowledge, he's never shared it with anyone." Theo sighed heavily. "There's nothing here. We should leave. I'll make a few calls when we return home."

"Of course." They headed toward the front door. He paused in the living room entryway and eyed the paintings hung on the walls. It occurred to him that a portrait or picture of Sebastian appeared nowhere in the entire apartment. Despite what he'd seen in the male's study, he had no clue what the guy looked like. And Theo hadn't offered a description of any kind. Why? Then again, why hide their real reason for coming here? Nothing about this evening made any bit of sense.

"Come along, Hamilton," his sire commanded.

"Sorry," he mumbled. Right. They were leaving. All of his unanswered questions would remain as such. At least for now. He needed to get to the library and see what he could find on his own. Maybe his research would even offer some insight into Theo's strange behavior.

Or force him to accept the inevitable. Vampires only looked out for themselves. No one else.

seven

Dear Miss Black,

While I appreciate your enthusiasm, I am currently unavailable to meet. However, I have enclosed a list of books I'm looking to add to the current collection. Once you've located any of the listed items, forward the details to me and I'll take care of the rest.

Regarding your recommendations, I concur with them. I'll be certain to pass them along to the general manager for immediate action.

Thank you for your hard work.

Sincerely,
Hamilton Morck

ODESSA READ OVER THE E-MAIL a third time. With a groan, she rolled her eyes. The simplicity of the benefactor's response shouldn't irritate her, yet it did. He hadn't tossed her suggestions aside as if they meant nothing, though it sounded that way. The male had refused to meet with her. His e-mail hadn't indicated he was *currently* unavailable, just that he was unavailable. She had no way to delve deeper into Hamilton Morck. Her gaze shifted from the computer to the steel filing cabinet.

Or did she?

It was a long shot. Administrators would've kept records for employees and any investors, but that may not include owners. She'd heard Hamilton Morck described a couple of ways. Maybe luck would be on her side tonight. Odessa rose from her chair, strode over to the filing cabinets, and opened the first drawer.

Nothing but employee files in that one. She skimmed over the last names. As expected, she didn't find anything. Without hesitation, Odessa shut that drawer and moved onto the second one. It contained files on books and things purchased for the lower level over the last year. Not what she was searching for, but it could prove useful.

She thumbed through the various folders and stopped on one a third of the way back. It wasn't labeled. Pursing her lips, she peered over her shoulder. No one was around. What could it hurt? Odessa pulled the file out, flipped it open, and narrowed her eyes. "What the hell?"

Dear Miss Bell,

While I appreciate your enthusiasm, I am currently unavailable to meet. However, I have enclosed a list of books I'd like you to procure. I have a few tomes recently purchased that I'll send to the library for the latest collection.

Regarding your recommendations for the preservation room, I will look into them. If there are any I agree with, then I'll be certain to pass them along to the general manager for immediate action.

As always, I appreciate all of your work on getting things established on the lower levels. I'm certain it will help put our little library on the map.

Sincerely,

Hamilton Morck

It sounded way too similar to the response she received. She brushed aside the word-for-word parts and turned the page. Another e-mail. "Interesting," she mumbled. Except this one came from Andrea Bell, the conservator who worked here before her. Odessa glanced over the sheet of paper and moved to the next one and the next.

This unmarked folder contained hundreds of e-mails back and forth between the previous conservator and Hamilton Morck. While they might provide some insight into the male, she couldn't spend all night reading them. There was another option. Not that she should. It was a supremely bad idea. Yet a good one, too.

Before she could talk herself out of it, she closed the drawer and packed the folder into her large, black purse. This wasn't why she'd kept it in here, but tonight it came in handy. She'd simply read the printed e-mails at home and return them tomorrow night. No one would even know they'd gone missing. Easy enough to handle.

Too bad they weren't what she'd hoped to find. Odessa returned to her search, scouring through each drawer. Though she didn't turn anything up, she refused to call it quits. A coworker of hers had mentioned a book a couple of days back. Reclaiming her seat at the computer, she called up their internal search engine. Instead of focusing on just Hamilton Morck, she typed in the surname alone.

Odessa blinked. That couldn't be right. Erasing her search, she tried again and received the same result. The book her coworker had referenced was in the preservation room. "Huh," she mumbled, and bit her bottom lip. Well, how about that? Quickly jotting the information down, she cleared out the search history and signed off the computer.

No one needed to see what she'd done. Would management view it as a fireable offense? Possibly, but best not to take any chances. She stood, left the office, and headed toward the elevator. Why hadn't Morgan told her about the location of the book? Everyone at the library knew why management had hired her. Then again, maybe that wasn't entirely accurate.

The reason for the last conservator's departure had gone unmentioned. Not that she'd bothered to question it. That information didn't seem all that important. Maybe the stack of e-mails she'd found offered an answer. Odessa tapped her foot. Had the elevator always taken this long? It dinged, and the door opened. "Finally."

She got on the elevator, pushed the button for the bottom floor, and folded her arms across her chest. It took forever for the door to shut. Fuck, why hadn't she taken the stairs? She could've gotten there faster. Odessa pinched the bridge of her nose. This really shouldn't bother her. Yet, it did. Why?

Running a hand through her hair, she let out a heavy sigh. That was a damn good question. It was simple. None of this had anything to do with the elevator. She blamed the e-mail Hamilton Morck had sent her. People had brushed her off in the past, but for this male…it had come so easily. It didn't help he shared a name with her late fiancé. Discovering something about the Morck family might help her separate them better.

That's what she yearned to find. No. She needed to find it. Because truthfully, Hamilton Morck sounded and looked like Hamilton Kring. But they had to be two different people. If they weren't…no, she couldn't even fathom the idea. It didn't matter that they had the same face. Or that Mr. Morck's brush-off reminded her of how Hamilton shrugged off her questions regarding his regular evening disappearances. *Hamilton Kring is dead,* she reminded herself. A mantra she repeated more and more these days.

The elevator door opened, letting her out onto the bottom floor. Without hesitating, she went straight to the preservation room, entered the security code, and walked into the room. She glanced at the sheet of paper in her hand and tapped her finger against her chin. "Alright. You should be…" her words trailed off as she approached the back wall. Odessa carefully scanned the markings on each spine.

"Aha!" She extracted the book from the stacks. Taking in a deep whiff of that musty scent she loved so much, she cracked it open. The author had recorded a family tree right in the front, which offered some insight all on its own. The line tracked back to the early 12th century. Certainly, further back than most, unless they used some kind of ancestry tool. But that didn't pique her interest. In the late 1700s a male in the family named Theodore started a tradition that carried his name forward. Each male child had the same name until Hamilton it appeared.

Odessa skimmed through the first few pages. One had a portrait of Theodore, the man who started the library. She'd seen it her first night on the main floor. It hung over a fireplace that served as a reading nook. Though this wasn't the Morck family's only business. They'd gotten started in banking, moved into importation and exportation, which they still ran today alongside the library. "That explains a few things."

"Explains what?"

Her gaze snapped over her shoulder. Shit. Had her subconscious summoned Hamilton's ghost? Yeah, he'd danced across her brain not mere moments ago, but this was becoming a habit. One she couldn't continue. Nor could she stop. Turning on the back of her heel, she faced him. Her cheeks heated a bit. "Just something I'm researching."

"Oh? Anything of interest?" He took a couple of steps toward her.

"Depends on your perspective." Why couldn't she just tell him? It wasn't like he was alive. The male she spoke to was nothing more than some image she'd conjured from her mind. Odessa pursed her lips. "I, um… this probably sounds ridiculous…not that you'd know the difference, but I'm looking into a family that…has just gotten me thinking about you a lot. I guess."

"That sounds…ominous."

"No, no. It's nothing like that." She shook her head. "I'm always thinking about you, especially being in a new place. Some days, all I wish for is that I could tell you everything I'm seeing and doing. Yeah, I can call you up like this…but it's not the same." He couldn't exactly reply to her with anything beyond what her subconscious imagined. Especially when she really needed his advice on how to handle things. Like how not to think about him so much without the constant reminder of his death.

"That doesn't mean you can't talk to me, Dess. You can tell me anything. I'll never judge you, but you know that."

Of course, she did. It was one of many things she loved about him. But this wouldn't compare to an actual conversation. An exchange between the two of them. Maybe she had to convince herself of that. "Except if I told you right now how much I miss you, then you'd respond with whatever my subconscious cooked up. Like how it's impossible to miss you when I always have you in my heart."

"You're only partially correct." Hamilton closed the distance between them. "I'd tell you how much I miss you, too." He reached out and caressed her cheek.

Odessa gasped and dropped the book in her hands. "I can feel you," she whispered. How was this possible? It shouldn't be. No matter how many times she'd conjured his image, nothing like this had ever happened. Unless… "Oh, God." Her eyes widened. Had she dreamed the entire night? The e-mail response and everything that followed?

Or was it so much worse than a simple dream? That had to be it. Her mind had finally turned against her. She backed up a couple of steps. "Oh, God, it's really happened," Odessa muttered and paced back and forth. "I've gone into a full-blown delusional psychosis. Just like my mother." She raked a hand through her long hair. Maybe if she focused on the sound of her heels as they clicked against the hardwood floor, her mind would snap back to reality.

Inhaling and exhaling several deep breaths, she repeated, *My fiancé is dead*, to herself. Odessa flicked her gaze to her hallucination of Hamilton. Shit. He still stood there. Though she could see his mouth move, no sound came out. "What? Why am I even talking to you? You're not really here."

Hamilton grabbed a hold of her arms and stopped her pacing. "Dess!"

The tightness of his grip burned a bit. Tears rolled down her cheeks.

This last year, she'd have given anything to notice these sensations any time his ghost haunted her. It hadn't occurred before now. What made this time different? "I've lost it," she mumbled in complete defeat.

"That's not true. You're the strongest woman I know." He cupped her cheek and brushed a kiss across her lips.

A shiver shot down her spine. She stared at Hamilton, holding the gaze of his piercing, dark-green eyes. Either she'd conjured an intense hallucination or something altogether different had happened. How was that even possible?

It wasn't. This was just her mind playing tricks on her, and she could prove it. That's what she had to do. Prove her brain wrong. Odessa pressed her lips to Hamilton's as she'd done so many times in the past. Oh, God. They were as soft and warm as she remembered. He swept his tongue across her bottom lip. Her lips parted ever so slightly, giving way for their tongues to entangle in a dance of passionate memories.

Her synapses lit up like the stars in the sky. She moaned into the kiss as he wrapped his arms around her, tightening the hold he had on her body. Oh, God. Even through the suit, every hard plane of his chest pressed against her. Something she'd never forgotten. No matter how much time had passed since…Odessa pulled out of his arms, breaking off the kiss. Lifting her fingers to her mouth, she attempted to stop the tingles that fired across her nervous system.

This isn't happening. I'm just imagining all of this. No matter how real it felt, she told herself. Not that she believed a single word. That kiss offered answers and brought up so many questions. How could any of this be possible? What was he? Certainly not the ghost she dreamed about. Somehow, he physically stood here in front of her. "How?" Despite all the questions dancing on her brain, she'd gotten only one out.

He dragged a hand down his face and sighed. "I can't answer that."

"Can't or won't?" she asked, although she already knew how he'd respond. Regardless of what had happened between them physically, nothing had truly changed. This was just like all of those nights she'd gone to bed alone, worried about him. Always worried—why should now be any different?

With a shake of his head, he closed the distance between them and gripped her shoulders tightly. Hamilton stared her directly in the eyes. "I'm sorry, Dess. I should've never kissed you. Not that you're going to remember any of this. You're going to forget I ever appeared tonight. Instead, you heard a noise that startled you and that's what caused you to drop the book. You'll go on about the rest of your night like normal."

If the glint in his green eyes was anything to go by, he truly believed what he'd just uttered. That somehow, she'd forget all that had just transpired. Her questions regarding him would simply disappear as if they'd never existed. It was utter bullshit. None of it would leave her mind at all. But maybe if she allowed him to think she accepted his story, then she could investigate on her own. And for the first time in the ten years since the day they'd met, she'd discover the truth.

"I'm going to forget. A noise startled me and I dropped the book," Odessa repeated.

Hamilton brushed a tender kiss across her forehead, backed up, and disappeared into thin air.

What the fuck? She bit the inside of her cheek to silence the gasp. Holy shit. What if he still hovered nearby? A chill ran down the length of her back as the door opened with a hiss. At least that answered one question. Odessa scanned the floor, located the book she'd dropped, and picked it up.

She had some digging to do.

eight

HAMILTON MAINTAINED HIS INVISIBILITY AS he followed Odessa off the subway at a distance. Despite the moment of lunacy he had last night, he refused to leave her side. After the kiss they'd shared, it seemed wise to keep some distance between them. All he could think about was doing it again. While his body cared little about the ensuing complications, should he do as he desired, his mind had other ideas.

Protect Odessa at all costs from vampires, even if that included him. If he was smarter, he would've tailed her from further back than thirty feet away. Except he barely tolerated that. Fuck, why had he kissed her? Things weren't perfect, but at least he could talk to her. Sort of. Not really.

It was all a mess. One he'd only made worse. Hamilton bit back a groan and melded his body against a cold, concrete column. Although he remained invisible, this time of morning, people bustled their way to work and lingered around the subway station. If he bumped into someone, he could unintentionally draw her attention. He'd already wiped her memory once. It wasn't something he wished to do again.

He scrunched his nose at the excessive amount of cologne wafting in the air from a nearby business professional. Not that it was enough to cover the stench of cigarette smoke coming off of them. It was more than enough to force him to move. Hamilton glanced at Odessa, barely catching sight of her backside as she ascended the staircase and exited the station. Shit. He wasn't supposed to lose sight of her.

Stepping from behind the column, he shoved his way through the gathering crowd and headed for the stairs. By the time he ran up them and reached the top, he'd completely lost sight of her. It shouldn't matter, except one vampire had already chased after her before. What was to prevent—?

A female's muffled scream hit his ears.

"Odessa!" Dropping his invisibility, Hamilton jumped the metal railing and darted around the corner toward the alley. He balled his fists up as he dove into the darkness and glared at the two thugs that had grabbed his fiancée. She struggled and fought against the tight hold the burly one had on her, though his grip didn't loosen any. Something that he would quickly change.

"Let her go!" he hissed.

"Nah, I think we'll hold on to her." The smaller male smirked and stepped forward, placing himself between Hamilton and the other guy.

"Bad move." Not that he had any problem plowing through one person or even two to get to his fiancée. Nothing would stop him from getting her to safety. If the erratic beating of their hearts and the copper scent of their blood were anything to go by, these two were human. Which meant one thing—he had to act carefully.

Leaving a trail of bodies in his wake would only draw unwanted attention. For both him and Odessa. He glanced at the male dragging her further back into the alley. Her breathing had become labored. A low growl rumbled deep in his chest. These idiots dared to hurt her. Hamilton charged at the runt, who surged toward him in return. The click of a switchblade tickled his ears. Which he easily dodged and countered with an uppercut, sending the male flying across the alley.

As the pissant landed atop a nearby dumpster, the burly thug tossed

Odessa against a brick wall with a loud thud. He bared his fangs. Not that it fazed the piece of shit. The lack of reaction surprised him a bit. That didn't matter. This guy would pay…hard.

Big man removed a large silver blade from his hip. They lunged at one another. The thug swiped at him, but he deflected the attack. Hamilton punched him. The guy stumbled a few feet back. Obviously, this one wouldn't go down as easily as the runt. Not that he'd used his full strength. He glimpsed Odessa out of the corner of his eye. His ears twitched at the faint sound of her breaths. She was alive, though knocked unconscious from what he sensed.

It was beyond time he dealt with this low-life. Hamilton feigned a right-hook, sidestepped to the left as the guy thrust his blade at him. Although the knife's edge caught him in the side, it didn't stop his momentum. He followed through with a knee to the gut, forcing the male back a couple of steps. But he was far from finished. Hamilton surged forward and slammed his forehead against the thug's face with a loud crunch. Blood splattered from the big man's nose.

The guy staggered backward. He stayed with him, punching him repeatedly. With every strike, more crimson covered his knuckles. Hamilton didn't cease until the thug fell to the ground. Better a bloody mess and alive than dead. Though, either worked for him at the moment. Shaking the thought off, he turned to where he'd seen Odessa. His gaze flicked briefly at the dumpster the runt had landed earlier as he strolled by it. One of them had gotten away.

Not that he had time to investigate the situation or dared to chase after the male. Odessa mattered the most right now. He crouched down, checked her breathing and pulse, and scooped her up into his arms. "I'm so sorry," Hamilton whispered, and brushed a kiss across her forehead. If he hadn't lost sight of her, **none of this would**'ve occurred.

Odessa groaned. Fuck, her head hurt. It throbbed like someone had used it as their own personal set of drums. What the hell had happened? She remembered leaving the subway station and walking toward home. That's when…she bolted upright. "Shit," she muttered.

"Take it easy," Hamilton said. "Lay back down. I've got a cold compress here."

Yeah, *that* happened. As if the kiss and his words last night hadn't revealed the truth, his presence earlier and here in front of her confirmed it. Somehow, her fiancé hadn't died.

Hamilton Kring was alive.

Although she had plenty of questions right now, she didn't dare ask a single one. Not when that sudden movement only intensified the pain radiating down her head and neck.

Following his suggestion, Odessa slowly lowered herself back down. She glanced around the room. At least she recognized this as her bedroom. Someone had pulled the deep-violet drapes she'd hung around the window shut. Something she would've done herself while she rested. The darkness sweeping across her bedroom eased the ache a bit. "What happened?"

Hamilton pressed a cold pack to her temple. "A couple of thugs attacked you."

"I remember that." Just like she recalled seeing him fly around the corner. Almost as if it hadn't existed. But she couldn't think too much about that now. Maybe as the pain ebbed a bit more, she could focus on what she truly wanted to know. Quiet didn't work for her either. Not when she needed answers like yesterday's news. "How did you end up there?"

"Does it really matter?"

Nope. She wasn't doing this. Keeping the compress against her head, Odessa sat up again. She slid back until her shoulders hit the bedframe. "When you've been dead for over a year…you're damn right it does."

Taken aback, his eyes widened. He scrubbed a hand down his face, let out a heavy sigh, and smirked. "You're a smart woman. I should've known you'd figure it out."

"How could I not when you kept appearing out of thin air?" Though she didn't know how many times he'd come to her as one of her visions. Or how often it was actually just her own mind at work. Regardless, she deserved the truth.

"That wasn't my intent."

"Then what was it? Or did you even have one?" She clenched her jaw to silence the litany of questions that threatened to spill forth. Hamilton would answer every single one of them, but she refused to rush through any of the thoughts running a hamster-wheel in her mind. Odessa pressed the cold-pack harder against her head. As if that would ease the torturous agony more.

"I don't know, Dess. It wasn't like I expected to see you again. When I did…everything rushed back to me. Our lives. Things we had planned." He leaned forward, digging his elbows into his thighs. "It was like seeing you for the first time all over again."

"Is that why you kissed me last night?" *Damn it,* she cursed herself under her breath. She hadn't meant to put that out there. Not since she'd convinced him she'd forgotten all about it. Too late to take it back. Maybe it was best they got everything out in the open.

Straightening up, he folded his arms across his broad chest. "You remember that?"

Did he seriously just get defensive with her? Odessa scoffed, tossed the compress aside, swung her legs off the bed, and rose to her feet. "You have a lot of nerve getting an attitude with me!" She shoved her finger in his face. "You were dead, Hamilton! Dead! Do you have any idea what you put me through? Yet, here you are, sitting there acting as if I'm in the wrong for pretending to heed your words." She stormed off.

He jumped to his feet and chased her. "I did that for your protection, Dess. It was the only way to keep you safe!"

"Like all the nights you left the house, refusing to tell me where you were going? Or lying about the bruises the next day? What? Didn't think I'd notice them?" Her heart thundered in her chest. Every unanswered question had just come out. As much as she tried to hold them back, she couldn't stop the truth from pouring out. She halted in her steps and spun on the back of her heel. "Was that about my safety, too?"

"Yes! That is all I've ever done."

Tears welled in the corner of her eyes. She desperately wanted to believe him. How could she? He'd hidden so much from her. Shaking her head, Odessa dismissed him with a flick of her hand. "And Claude thought it would be a good idea I move here," she snickered.

"What?" Hamilton snapped. "My uncle Claude? He suggested you move?"

Odessa glowered at Hamilton. Just when she thought for one second, she had a handle on the rage lighting up her synapses. "Seriously? That's what bothers you? Not anything else that I've said or questioned? Why the fuck does it matter what brought me to New York?"

"Because he's the one who killed me!"

She blinked, opened her mouth, and snapped it shut. No way she just heard him right. The man was a weasel, but she'd never seen him as a murderer. Of course, that would also suggest that Hamilton was…dead. Odessa swallowed to wet her parched throat. She bit the inside of her cheek, inhaled and exhaled a deep breath, and clenched and released her fists. "You need to tell me everything, Hamilton. The complete truth. Now."

He gripped the back of his neck. "Fine, but only if you sit. You got thrown against a building, Dess. You shouldn't be up stomping around."

Odessa crossed her arms and narrowed her eyes at him. The way he spoke to her made it seem like no time had passed at all. It didn't matter if they both knew differently. Or if his words held some truth. "Then I suggest you get me a stiff drink. I get the feeling I'm going to need it."

"That's not really…alright." He winced. "I can, uh, do that. Where do you keep the liquor?"

"Top shelf. Far left cabinet." Odessa turned on her heel, stalked down the hall, and passed the entertainment system as she headed straight for the couch. A subtle pounding had returned with a vengeance. This is what she got for getting pissed on top of a headache.

"Good to know some things won't change," Hamilton mumbled as he disappeared into the kitchen.

Had he expected everything to remain the same? Life didn't work like that. People grew, so naturally, change followed. That was a conversation for another time. "That doesn't sound like an explanation." She sat on the sofa, tucking one leg under her bottom, as her kitten jumped up onto the cushion and climbed into her lap.

He leaned on the countertop, peering at her through the space beneath the hanging cabinets. "Where would you like me to start?"

The beginning seemed best, but then this could take forever. She wanted straight answers from him. "If you're dead, how are you standing here talking to me?"

"Come on, Dess. You already know the answer to that. You've seen the books I've used for research. Both at the library and before…well, my death."

No. That was impossible. All of those books referenced things of myth—vampires, shapeshifters, witches…they didn't exist. Then again, Hamilton shouldn't either. She'd seen the state of his corpse. Yeah, they had a closed casket funeral because of it, but…the painting. Odessa scoffed. "So…you're telling me Hamilton Kring died and was reborn as Hamilton Morck?"

"Yes." He stepped into the living room and set a bottle of gold liquid on the coffee table next to two empty glasses. "Unbeknownst to me, the night Claude killed me, I had vampire blood in my system. Don't ask how it got there because honestly, I don't know. My sire hasn't shared that bit of information with me. All I know is that he was there at the hotel when I awoke about thirty miles outside of Solvang."

His sire? Although she understood the terminology, it was a lot for her to wrap her mind around. The author hadn't mentioned vampiric suspicions in the book on the Morck family. That didn't make it impossible. The family tree and portraits she'd noticed in the work were questionable. "Let me guess…Theodore Morck." It made the most sense. Despite the difference in facial hair, the male relatives all looked the same.

Hamilton cocked an eyebrow at her as he poured her a glass and held it out to her. "That's right. How'd you know?"

Odessa wrapped her hand around the glass, her fingers brushing against his. Their gazes locked on one another. The skin of her face and neck flushed as warmth flooded her body and her heart pounded in her chest. God, it had gotten hot in here. Shoving the sensations aside, she cleared her throat. "I, uh, did some research…on the Morck family."

"The book you had last night," he mumbled with a slight shake of his head. "I suppose that shouldn't surprise me."

"No, it shouldn't." She tore her gaze from his, pulled the glass from his hand, nearly sloshing some of the sweet nectar out as she did. Not that she wished to waste a single ounce of it. Especially given the insanity of their conversation. She took a sip and gripped the glass tightly with both hands. Best way to keep herself from doing something stupid.

"Right." After pouring himself a glass, Hamilton sat at the other end of the couch. "Theo brought me to his home here. Where I've dedicated myself to learning everything I can about vampires."

Silence stretched between them as she sipped more of the Tequila. Could it all really be that simple? That life existed outside of the natural order? Except, how did that apply to witches and shapeshifters? Something about it all didn't quite add up. There were so many myths and legends regarding the creation and existence of such creatures. How could anyone tell which was right? Odessa knocked back the last of her drink and poured herself another.

"Dess…please say something."

"What exactly do you want me to say? Am I just supposed to suddenly be okay? For the last year, I believed you were dead. I mourned you… spent endless nights…" No. She couldn't go there. If she even thought about the anguish, the tears would start all over again. The day he'd died, he'd taken a part of her with him. She'd become a shell of the woman that once existed. One that used work as a diversion. Just so she wouldn't have to feel the pain that accompanied the loss.

Except now, it was more than that. They'd spent nine years together. He had all that time to share his truth. He'd researched these creatures prior to his death. Known about them.

How many times had she spotted books around their apartment on mythological beings? That was the problem. Wasn't it? She gulped down half of her second drink. Not that it ended there. Her gaze dropped to the floor as she finished the other half of Tequila in her glass. "We crossed paths my first night at the library. You admitted as much." Odessa stared at him, briefly giving him a moment to deny the truth. It was only part of what she needed to know. "When was the first time you spoke to me?"

Hamilton sipped the drink in his hand, set the glass on the table, and sighed. "A few nights ago. After your, uh…date."

Of course. The night she'd pulled out one of their photo albums and reminisced about their engagement. The more they talked, the angrier she got. But this was far from over. She refused to quit when there was so much more for her to find out. If only the alcohol helped. "How long have you known about these…things?"

"Dess—"

"How long?" she hollered. Her blood boiled in a way she'd never known possible. In all the time they'd spent together, not once had she ever desired to slap him. Or even throw an empty glass at him. Both crossed her mind at that moment.

His dark-green eyes dropped to the wooden floor. "My whole life," he replied, his voice just above a whisper.

Shifting her gaze to the ceiling, Odessa inhaled and exhaled a deep breath. Not that it did a damn thing to ease the red she saw. Her grip on the glass tightened. Bard meowed at her. The kitten's presence settled the pounding inside her chest. Not much, but enough. She placed the glass on top of the coffee table. "Did you ever plan to tell me?"

"I don't know." Hamilton ran a hand through his chocolate-brown coiffed hair. "Dess, I wanted to protect you. Keep you away from the darkness of my world for as long as possible."

There was that word again—protect. Though it sounded like a friendly word to use, it also sounded like she couldn't *protect* herself. Something she'd done for years before they even met. Or had he always viewed her as something fragile? Something easily broken? "Did your mother know? Claude?"

He blew out a heavy breath, hung his head, and clasped his hands at the back of his neck. "Claude was born into it as a hunter…like I was. As for my mother…" He lifted his gaze to her. "That was my father's choice, but, yes…she knew."

"Get out," Odessa said through gritted teeth. Removing the kitten from her lap, she cradled him in her arms and stood. Though he hadn't explained the term *hunter,* she didn't require it. Everything finally lined up. It all made perfect sense. The number of times she'd found books for him, translated passages, and helped him with research all synced together.

"I can't leave."

"Oh, yes, you can. If you need some help, there's the door!" She pointed at it. Not that he could miss it. She'd happily show it to him if he so deemed it necessary.

"You don't understand, Dess…I can't." He rose to his feet, strode over to the window covered by another set of dark-violet drapes. Hamilton inched a portion of one drape aside. Sunlight streamed through, reflecting off the wooden floor. He held his hand out for a split second in the sun. His skin sizzled, and he yanked his hand back. "Like I said. I can't."

Odessa blinked. It was one thing to hear him say it, but another to see the proof. Not just as the sun physically hurt him, but as every part of his hand stitched itself back together. Almost as if it hadn't even happened. Though her anger dissipated, it didn't change her mind much. She shook her head, sidestepped the coffee table, and started toward the hallway.

"Dess—"

"No!" She spun around to face him. Tears pricked the corners of her eyes, threatening to spill over. "You do not get to do this to me! You had years, Hamilton! Years! To tell me the truth. We were getting married, for fuck's sake. And I'm just what…supposed to roll over and accept that you did the *right* thing?" With a shake of her head, Odessa scoffed. "You didn't. So, if you can't leave, then fine. But you can stay the hell out here because right now, I can't even look at you."

"I'm sorry, Dess. I never wanted to hurt you."

"Except you did. Your lies have tainted every memory we share. Everything good about our relationship…it's gone." That wasn't true, but she refused to delve into those emotions. They were dangerous. Odessa turned toward the hallway and glanced over her shoulder at him. "For the record, I hope that was pure agony. Then you might understand a fraction of the hell you put me through." She walked off, heading straight for her bedroom.

nine

HAMILTON STARED OUT THE WINDOW of the town car as it headed down the long driveway leading to the manor. His sire returned with him to meet with the council. While part of him focused on the issue that lay ahead, the other half could think of nothing but Odessa. After the sun set last night, he'd done as she asked and given her space. Though it had proven more difficult than he expected to stay away. Especially after spending a day in silence around her. He hoped their time apart would suffice. Once this was over, he planned to visit her at work.

"Are you certain you know what you're doing?" Theo asked.

"Yes," he responded. The last twenty-four hours gave him more than enough time to come up with a solution. Something he believed the council wouldn't refuse. He owed much of the idea to his fiancée. Not that he suspected she'd realize the valued information she'd unintentionally shared. Of course, he knew things she didn't. That made all the difference.

But it wasn't the only thing he thought about.

"Did you sleep well?" Hamilton asked as he plated the meal he'd spent the last thirty minutes preparing. It seemed like a good idea as she showered. A way to ease into what remained of the difficult conversation they'd started

that morning. Though he hoped it wouldn't end the same way. Not that Odessa responded to him as she moved about the kitchen, preparing herself a cup of coffee.

Maybe if he tried another tactic.

"I made your favorite breakfast. A three-cheese, egg-white omelet with spinach and ham." He carried two plates over to the dining room table he'd set to perfection, including a pair of lit candles. Though given the silence and how she ignored him, he might have gone over the top.

Odessa stepped around him, sat at the table, and placed her mug down above the plate. Without so much as a word, she picked up her fork and took a bite of the omelet.

"Alright," he muttered and claimed his own seat. Obviously, the night wouldn't go much better than the day. All day he'd sat around her apartment as she hunkered down in her bedroom, hidden away from him. Even the few times she'd appeared in the hallway or kitchen, she hadn't so much as looked his way. Now, nothing but quiet surrounded them. At no point over their nine years together had he ever upset her this much.

If she'd acted that way to teach him a lesson, he'd learned it. Having her in reach, yet so far out of reach, tortured him. That kind of pain surpassed the sting of the sun yesterday morning. Something he demonstrated simply to get her to see the truth. It ended up showing him something instead.

The town car eased to a stop in front of the manor's main entrance. Hamilton adjusted the buttons of his coat and climbed out of the vehicle. He could've waited for Grayson to open his door, but he had more important things on his agenda. This was merely a step in that direction.

"You seem rather confident. What is this plan you have?"

"Nothing you need to worry over." He hadn't shared any part of his thought process with his sire. Not even to confirm his beliefs regarding the council's reaction to his proposition. Something deep down told him it wasn't necessary. Besides, it wasn't as if Theo had shared everything with him. Why shouldn't secrets go both ways? The only person he intended to tell about all of this was Odessa. He wouldn't keep anything from her ever again.

"I hope you don't intend to do anything drastic. Or attempt to plead your case. Without Sebastian around, that isn't an option either of us has."

"Not at all." Hamilton snickered. How could he depend on someone he'd never met? Simple. He couldn't. With a shake of his head, he strolled forward, eyed the knocker, and rang the doorbell. It chimed loudly, easily notifying all in residence of their arrival. Unlike they had a couple of days ago, they'd gotten here several minutes early. A habit his father had taught him at a young age.

A moment later, the same male as before answered the door. "Lord Morck. Mr. Morck." He bowed his head to them and stepped aside, opening the door wider. "Please, come in."

"Thank you." At least the guy addressed him this time. Last time, the butler looked right through him as if he didn't even exist. Hamilton passed by the servant, strolled through the foyer, and headed toward the enormous library. Unless someone stopped him, he assumed their meeting would follow the previous course. Though he took more time as he strode down the hallway. Last time, he hadn't paid much attention to the paintings hung on the wall. He did this time around. A few of them looked familiar.

About halfway down hung a portrait of Isaac, leader of the Élan Clan. No one could ever mistake those mahogany eyes for anyone else. The male certainly embodied the prided intellect of his clan. In the painting anyway. Hamilton scoured it for a date. He found nothing more than the year 1818. Good to know.

Two paintings to its left hung a portrait of Ashton, leader of the Mezmæ Clan. Another that no one could ever mistake for someone else. The male had long, midnight-black hair pulled back into a ponytail, significant to the time of the portrait, steel-blue eyes that emblazoned lust and desire, and a chiseled jawline for everyone to envy. His appearance hadn't changed much since the…jeez…17th century. None of them looked beyond their early 20s at best. How could the guy have lived over three hundred years?

Hamilton shook his head and eyed the portrait hanging next to the library door. It was of the only other clan leader who'd spoken last time: Devereaux, leader of the VēlM Clan. A group known for their empathic abilities. No wonder the guy had figured out so much about Odessa. Yeah, he needed to do more homework on the different clans. More than what he'd already done. Glancing over his shoulder at Theo, he nodded to his sire. Time to see just how much the male trusted him.

They entered the meeting room and stopped a few feet from the platform where all the clan leaders sat. Only six clan leaders occupied the chairs. One seat remained empty. Just as he expected. Not that it would hurt him or alter his plan. Hamilton clasped his hands at the small of his back, bowed low, showing his deference and respect, and straightened as previously instructed. "My lords."

"I take it you have come to a decision, Mr. Morck," Isaac stated as he steepled his fingers together.

"Yes." He left it at that. They'd decided his punishment so easily, it seemed only fair to make them wait for his answer.

Isaac tapped his fingers on his knee. "What is it?"

"A counter-proposal. While I'm sure all of you believe you've thought through the options you gave me, I whole-heartedly disagree. If you'll hear me out, I've come up with something that will benefit all of us." Theo had warned him many times how it wouldn't serve either of them if the council discovered the truth regarding his history. Though he was certain Isaac hadn't gotten into his head, nothing could convince him that Devereaux hadn't picked up anything about his past. Or his family. He had to take advantage of his suspicions, whether or not they were true.

"That isn't—"

Devereaux held up a hand, cutting Isaac off. "I'd like to hear his offer."

"Very well," Isaac grumbled. "Pray tell, what is your proposal?"

Hamilton took a couple of steps forward. "I have it on good authority there is a hunter in town. A rather good one. However, I'm aware of his…

tactics and I believe it behooves all of us if I use that knowledge to present him to you. Dead or alive. Your choice." If his uncle could betray him, it seemed only right to return the favor. Especially if it spared Odessa's life.

Silence fell across the lot of them. Though none of them spoke, each of the clan leaders shared glances at one another. Isaac rested his elbow on the chair's arm and shifted his gaze to Theo. "Do you know of whom he speaks?"

"Yes, I believe I do."

Devereaux draped one leg elegantly over the other and folded his hands in his lap. His steel gaze focused intently on Hamilton. "You would betray your own kind to protect this woman? She is that important to you?"

Well, that confirmed at least part of his theory. While he didn't have the details, the council knew the truth of his heritage. No reason to hide any part of it now. "I don't see him as *my kind,* but I'd do anything to keep Odessa safe. As you said, she's the love of my life. So, yes, she's *that* important to me."

"I see," Devereaux replied. He dipped his chin at Isaac and turned his attention back to Hamilton. "We accept your counter-offer Mr. Morck. We prefer you bring him back alive, though his head will suffice. You have three days."

"Three days?" Hamilton repeated.

"My Lord," Theo interjected. "What my protégé is attempting to say is that three days hardly seems enough time to locate a hunter of such prowess. We humbly request for more time. Two weeks should be sufficient."

"We shall not award such boldness." Devereaux steepled his fingers together and steeled his gaze at Hamilton. "Ten days. If you don't provide either in that timeframe, then the female and your sire will die. Understood?"

Also, something he expected. Not that he'd allow it to happen. He'd present them with Claude's head and have this whole punishment nonsense done and over with. "Understood."

"Excellent. Then I suggest you get started." Devereaux waved them off with a dismissive hand.

"Of course." Hamilton bowed to them one last time before he and his sire departed. Neither spoke, even once they'd gotten in the car. Which made everything better. Now he could get to the rest of his evening.

Odessa rubbed her eyes and groaned. Who knew so many vampire origins existed? She had seven books scattered across the table, each with its own version of how vampires came about. These didn't even include the eight she'd pored over last night. She thought the time away from Hamilton would've done some good. Instead, it only sent her mind into a deeper tailspin.

"That good, huh?"

Shit. When had he gotten here? How had she missed the door opening? She glanced over her shoulder at him. For a dead guy, Hamilton looked damn good. Three-piece suits did wonders for him. Though it left a few things to the imagination, the slacks hugged his legs like jeans hadn't ever done. She really shouldn't notice something like that. With a huff, Odessa turned her attention back to the tomes in front of her. "I thought we agreed you'd give me space."

"We did." He strode over to the table, pulled out a chair, and sat next to her. "But I have to talk to you."

She peered over at him. He had an old book in his hands, one that was rough around the edges. Its pages appeared a bit frayed, but it was still in one piece. That said something about its age. "Does it have something to do with that?" She gestured to the tome.

"Yes, and no. I brought this as a peace offering." He held it out to her. "I figured you had a lot of questions. Judging by the table, you're not getting much of anywhere."

"How are there so many theories about the creation of vampires? And how do you even tell which one is real? Or is it just some small part of each of them is valid?" she blurted out before she could even stop herself. These were all things she could've asked him if she hadn't vowed to dig into it on her own. Too late to take it all back. Maybe one day, it would prove useful.

"Every culture has their own version. I mean…" his words trailed off as he glimpsed across the scattered books. Hamilton selected one and pulled it close. "Take this one, for example. It's the Egyptian myth describing Sekhmet as the oldest vampire. The only truth to this is the desire for blood. That's the thing. Something about what each book dictates will be based on accuracy. The hard part is deciphering between it all. Usually, the best way is to look for commonalities in the references."

Commonalities. It made perfect sense. That's why he'd collected so many books on the subject. Except, wouldn't he already know about the creation of vampires? She raised an eyebrow at him. "So, if this isn't true, except for some small part, then why do you have it?"

"I've spent the last year purchasing whatever tomes I could get my hands on because I hoped they might point me to…a cure."

Odessa blinked and replayed his response in her mind. Wow! Not an answer she saw coming. Yet, it made sense. Some of these volumes had mentioned hunters. Those books offered her the most insight. Though she hadn't read anything about a cure. "Is that even possible?"

"I don't know," he admitted. "My sire keeps telling me to give up the search, but…I'm not ready to quit looking yet. However, that's not something we need to discuss." Hamilton pushed a few of the books aside and set the one in his hand in front of her. "Here."

Her gaze settled on the tattered tan cover. It had no title on the front. Nothing to denote what it spoke about. She flipped the book open and eyed the markings written on the first few pages. "Is this…Aramaic?"

"Yes, but how did you know that? I didn't think you spoke it."

"I don't…at least not fluently. I've only recently started learning it." Out of her periphery, she caught him frowning. What did he expect? That she'd spent every day of the last year mourning him? Odessa shrugged. "I had a lot of time on my hands. It was best that I stay busy." Less of a chance her mind would take quick trips all leading to him.

"Right. Well, uh, this deals mostly with hunters, but it also addresses the origin of each species—witches, shapeshifters, vampires, and hunters. I thought it might help answer any of your questions."

"Thank you. That's…thoughtful." Try as she might, she couldn't deny that truth. Nor could she deny he'd always had her best interest at heart, no matter how mad she was with him. Chewing on the inside of her cheek, she let out a small sigh and turned her chair toward him. "I'm sorry for yelling at you yesterday. I just…this is all a lot for me to take in."

Hamilton clasped her hand. "You don't have to apologize, Dess. You have every right to be upset with me. I've kept a lot from you, but I want to change all of that. If you'll give me a chance."

Tingles shot down her spine. The warmth of his skin against hers lit her synapses up like the night sky. She cleared her throat. "I can, uh, do that. Just promise me something."

"Anything."

"Don't hold any of it back. Good or bad, I want to know. And please, please, don't try to convince me it's in my head. That hurts just as much as you keeping secrets." Possibly more. Although they hadn't talked about it, he knew the fear she'd faced over the years. Especially with what happened to her mother.

"I know. I'm sorry about that, Dess. I…" He shook his head. "No. There's no excuse for it." Hamilton brushed a tender kiss to her forehead, squeezed her hand, and stroked the back of his knuckles across her cheek. "I promise to tell you everything and not to treat you like it's just your imagination."

She leaned into his touch. God, she'd missed it so much. With this agreement between them, they should do something to truly seal it. Like a kiss. Odessa bit her bottom lip. That was such a bad idea. Their gazes met. All sense of propriety disappeared. Their lips fused together. She swept her tongue along the seam of his mouth. Their tongues entangled in an epic battle as Hamilton wrapped his arms around her and the kiss deepened.

The hard plane of his chest pressed against her breasts. Her nipples pebbled beneath her silky blouse, intensifying the electricity humming through her body. Nothing about this could be wrong. Not when her heart beat so loudly in her ears.

Hamilton broke off the kiss and released the hold he had on her. "I'm sorry, Dess. I, uh…" He rose to his feet, putting space between them, and crossed over to a bookcase. "That's not why I came here. I came here… so we could talk."

Did he seriously just apologize for kissing her when she initiated it? "Right." He had to have known it would happen. They had a lot of history between them. As angry as she'd gotten with him, her heart had also filled with relief. How could the desire to touch or kiss not exist between them? Odessa folded her arms across her chest and narrowed her eyes at him. "You know what, no. I don't accept your apology because I won't apologize for kissing you. It's only natural. But if you just want to talk…then far be it from me to stop you."

His gaze shifted to her. He scratched his cheek, opened his mouth, and snapped it shut. "Um…" Hamilton leaned his elbow on a shelf. "Do you, uh…?" his voice cracked. He visibly swallowed. "I, uh, think…Claude might be in town."

Really? That's what he wanted to talk about—his uncle? Not a topic she would've chosen. "What makes you say that?"

"I think he knows the truth about me." A frown settled across his face. "Let me back up a second. Last night, I returned to the alley where those thugs grabbed you. I wanted to see if I could find anything left behind." Hamilton dug into the front pocket of his dark-blue slacks and presented a motel matchbook. "It could be nothing, but I checked this place out. While I didn't locate my uncle, it was seedy enough to be someplace he'd stay."

"Okay." A dodgy part of town didn't offer much in evidence. Not that they'd bring this to the police. There had to be more to go on than something so insignificant. "That just sounds like a lot of supposition based on his prior attempt on your life."

"Something about those men felt…off. Or at least one of them." He tucked the matchbook back into his pocket. "I revealed my vampiric face to the one that had a hold of you. It didn't affect him. And he had the right weapon to hurt me. Made me question if…someone told him what to expect."

His conclusion sounded more logical now. Though she still couldn't get it all to add up. She pursed her lips. "My dad said Claude was out of town. But that doesn't mean Claude is here."

"If you're trying to convince me he's not, that doesn't help." Hamilton crossed one ankle over the other. "It only solidifies my belief. Which leads me to my true purpose here. I want you to stay at the manor with my sire and I." He lifted a hand, silencing her objection. "At least until I find and kill my uncle."

"There are so many things wrong with that statement." Odessa turned and shut the book in front of her. She stood, closed a few of the others, and picked them up. Talking while she returned them to their rightful location would ease the tension in her shoulders. "First off, I'm not upending my life again. I can accept you as a vampire, even your life as a hunter, but I'll be damned if I allow it to force me into anything I don't choose for myself. Second, kill your uncle? Are you fucking serious right now?"

"Yes, I am. Before you go into a spiel about it, let me explain."

"Fine." She stopped in front of the table, clutching a tome close to her chest. "Explain."

"The vampire council gave me a choice of punishment. Neither option was viable, so I made a counter-offer, which they accepted. But it means I have to kill my uncle. Given everything he's taken from me, I'm well within my rights, but that has nothing to do with why I'm going after him."

"Then why? What could be so important that you'd actively choose to kill him?" Just because she believed Claude was a weasel didn't mean he deserved to die.

Hamilton pushed off the bookcase and took a few steps in her direction. "Your life."

"Oh," she replied. What else could she say? How had her name even come up to the council? Did that mean they wanted her dead? Why? What the hell had she done? So many questions. Not that she wished to have him answer a single one. Odessa slumped against the table. "I…uh…"

"Hey." He closed the distance between them and gently lifted her chin with his forefinger. "I promised to tell you everything. Maybe we save the rest of this for tomorrow."

"Uh, yeah. That sounds like a good idea." This had quickly become a bit too much for her. So much that every bone in her body weighed her down. Or maybe the tension had gotten that extreme. Either way, she had to figure this out. And just how much she desired to be a part of it.

Ten

"TO A LONG OVERDUE MEAL." Odessa lifted her wine glass and clinked it against her friend's glass. It wasn't the best of toasts, but Lucy didn't seem to notice. That was a good thing because after the last couple of nights, she desperately needed to talk. Not that she had any clue how to broach the topic of Hamilton.

"I'll drink to that," Lucy commented. She sipped the Merlot from her glass. "This is such a good place to have an early dinner."

"This was definitely a good idea." Odessa glanced around the restaurant, taking it all in. From the mustard-hued walls to the red-velvet banquettes, none of it was what she imagined when her friend suggested they meet at the Blue Ribbon Brasserie.

"Though I'm sure you didn't call me to talk about the food or wine. No matter how good it is."

"You know me so well. Um, I don't know. I guess…New York just isn't what I expected." Far from it, actually. She cracked a faint smile, sipped her wine, and set the glass on the table.

"It's just a different lifestyle. Busier than what you're used to. Give it time. I promise it'll get easier."

"It's not that," Odessa muttered. "I mean, yes, things move faster here, but it's not what's…throwing me off." She chewed on her bottom lip. God, was she really going to do this? Tell her best friend about what happened with Hamilton? Except, what if other vampires went after Lucy because of that knowledge? What if Lucy told her father? The two of them might have her committed.

"Oh, my God. I know that look! You met someone!" Lucy squealed and clasped Odessa's hands. "I'm so happy for you!"

"Well…" her words trailed off. How the fuck did she answer that? In some small way, it was true. Just not how one might think. Removing her hands from her best friend's grasp, she picked up her glass, took a big gulp of wine, and tilted her head. "What look? I don't get a look."

"Yes, you do." Lucy chuckled. She picked up her glass and took a sip of wine. "Anytime you're trying to avoid a conversation or talking about a crush, your face scrunches, your eyes twinkle, and you chew on your bottom lip. I *still* remember the first time I ever saw that look. So, come on. Out with it. Who's the guy?"

Odessa frowned. Did she seriously get a look? No. That couldn't be right. Not that it mattered. Lucy had figured out she had something to talk about. She just couldn't go blabbing anything about Hamilton. Maybe there was a way around that. "Alright, fine. You got me. I might have met someone."

Their server returned to the table and set down the platter of cheese fondue they'd ordered. "Is there anything else I can get for you ladies at the moment?"

Lucy glanced at Odessa. "No, thank you. We're good."

"Of course." He dipped his chin in acknowledgment and left.

"Now, do I have to ask again, or are you going to give me something to go on?" Her best friend picked up a skewer and started in on the platter.

"His name is Austin, and he lives in my building." Although she used her neighbor's information, she could still get Lucy's opinion on things. She just had to do one thing—lie. Sort of. None of her concerns really applied to him. Some of it might be hard to swallow. She'd only gone on one date with the guy. As much as she wished otherwise, Lucy could read her really well. Not that it was a bad thing. In most cases. It would be so much better if she could just tell her best friend the truth. Except danger would likely follow. Here, lying was better.

"Well, I like the sound of him already. What kind of work does he do? Lawyer? Real estate? Oh, doctor? That would be nice."

Odessa snickered. Because those were the only options, right? She snaked a skewer, stabbed an apple slice, and dipped it in cheese. "Remind me again, how are you single?"

"By choice." Lucy plucked a piece of cheese-covered apple from the metal stick with her teeth.

"Right," she drew the word out. They both knew that wasn't true. The woman went through men like she did a spin class. Lucy's shoes lasted longer than her relationships. Odessa had witnessed one male that had put her best friend through an array of emotional baggage in a matter of three days. Talk about a rollercoaster ride from hell.

"How did this become about my relationships? Weren't we talking about your new beau?"

"We went on one date. He's definitely not mine. Nor my type, really. More yours." So what, if she deflected a little? It was better to play on what she could than talk about what she couldn't. Then again, maybe there was a way to discuss it without mentioning everything else. Odessa took another sip of wine, yet held onto the glass. "Do you ever feel like the world is hiding this big secret from you?"

Lucy's eyebrows furrowed as she leaned back in her chair. "What's going on, Dess?"

She dropped her gaze to the table and set her glass down. "I found an old journal of Hamilton's while unpacking the other day. And it just…" her words trailed off. "He was hiding things from me."

"What? Are you sure? I mean…that doesn't really sound like him."

"Yeah." Odessa lifted her eyes to her best friend. "He had this whole other life, Luce. I didn't know a thing about it. Makes me feel like a fool." No truer words had ever left her mouth. How could she trust him again? Something she had to figure out. Or truly let him go forever. How could she do that when she still loved him? Which sounded just as baffling as his vampirism.

"Seriously? Like another woman? Secret child? A whole family?" Lucy shook her head. "He always seemed so strait-laced to me. I guess you never really know someone."

Yeah, there was a lot she hadn't known about him. Not that any of those applied. "No. Just…family secrets." Though it didn't explain as much as she expected. His mother and uncle's relationship, for one. Those two had married only a few months after his father passed. Who did that kind of thing? Was that normal for hunters? Odessa finished the last of the wine in her glass. Shit. That hadn't lasted as long as she'd hoped.

"That's it?"

"You say that like it's not a big deal." Maybe explaining things this way didn't work out how she imagined. Or had she actually gone over the top? No. No way she'd overreacted about any of this. Hamilton had lied to her for the entirety of their relationship.

"Well…I mean, his family has never been normal. Even if they looked that way, you never know what's happening behind closed doors." Her best friend skewered another apple slice, dipping it in the fondue. "I mean…how long did it take you to tell him about your mother?"

Odessa let out an exasperated sigh. As much as she hated to admit it, Lucy had a point. Certain pieces of information regarding her family's… history…she hadn't wanted to share. Her father had convinced her it was the right thing to do. "Years," she grumbled. Not that it changed the way Hamilton looked at her. It had only brought them closer together.

Their server swung by their table. "How is everything tasting?"

"Excellent," Lucy replied.

"Would you care for another glass of Merlot?" He gestured toward Odessa's empty glass.

"Yes, thank you." Another glass wouldn't hurt her any or even get her tipsy. Not with all the food they still had coming their way. She handed the glass over to him.

"Of course." With a dip of his chin, he left the table.

"Then why does it surprise you Hamilton had secrets about his family?" Lucy posed. "Or is it just because…well, you can't ask him why he hid it?"

"Since when did you become so level-headed?" Odessa frowned. Not that Lucy had a temper, but this didn't sound like the female she remembered. At least not completely. "Don't think I've forgotten how much you used to remind me I could do better."

Lucy tapped her chin. "Mmm, I don't ever remember saying that."

Chewing on the inside of her bottom lip, Odessa pressed a forefinger to the side of her temple. It helped silence the slight throbbing in her head. Her friend would suggest she made something so idiotic up. But why lie about it? Unless…she snickered. "You're teasing me."

Lucy smirked as she picked up her glass. "I'm just trying to get you to lighten up." The woman took a sip of wine. "Look, you know I love you, but you can't let the past eat away at you like this. Please, don't try to object. I can see clear as day what it's doing. Just let it be. You've gone on a date with what sounds like a dreamy guy, yet…the past has your attention."

"I love Hamilton," Odessa admitted. She blinked as she sat up a little straighter in the chair. This was the first time in months she'd uttered those words aloud. Even with all she'd discovered in the last few days, her feelings for him hadn't altered. A soft smile crossed her face. That didn't mean she could act as if he was alive. "I know he's gone, Luce. That it's been over a year, but those feelings don't just go away. They'll always be there. And if I'm honest with myself, I'm not ready to be with someone new."

"That's okay, Dess." Lucy grinned, rested her elbows on the table, and leaned forward. "Look, I know what kind of love you and Hamilton shared. Yes, there were times I thought you could do better, but I also saw how much you grew with him. He changed you. Not in a bad way. You were stronger and more confident with him. He brought this light out in you. This is the first time I've seen it since his passing. I hope it stays."

There was something about him. Something that made her feel more… herself. Almost as if…she was home. "I don't plan to let it go anywhere."

"Good. Because that would be a shame."

"Yes, it would." Maybe she didn't have all the answers, but at least she had a direction forward. Though, figuring some parts out would prove interesting. Their server returned to the table with her second glass of Merlot. Another arrived just behind him with their food. Perfect timing. Hopefully, it would give her all the fuel she needed to sort the rest of the mess out in her head. Without dumping it all on her best friend. Lucy didn't deserve the trouble that came with it.

Hamilton brushed his fingers along the violet comforter on Odessa's bed as he strolled toward the hallway. "Dess?" he called out. He probably should've used her front door, but it was better to climb through her window. Less of a risk of someone spotting him. His presence already put her in enough danger. If he could avoid adding more, he would.

As he rounded the corner into the hallway, Bard meowed at him. "Hey, little guy." He crouched down on the back of his haunches and held out his hand. The black kitten rubbed up against his fingers. "Don't suppose your mama is somewhere around, is she?"

The silence that filled the rest of the apartment suggested Odessa hadn't yet returned home. Meant he had no choice but to be patient. Hamilton picked up the kitten, who snuggled in closer. His ears perked up at the footsteps that echoed in the outer hall. Who could that be? They were too heavy to be Odessa's. Unless…no, Claude wouldn't do something so reckless. If the male came by Odessa's place, he'd sneak in somehow.

A knock sounded from the other side of the door. It wouldn't hurt to see who was visiting. Hamilton strode down the hallway and headed for the front door. He flipped the bolt and cracked it open. His eyes narrowed at the blond-headed male in front of him. The one she'd gone out with. "Can I help you?"

"Oh, um, I…" the male's words trailed off as he backed up a step. "I was, uh, looking for Odessa. This is her place, right?"

Hamilton set the kitten down on the floor. He stepped out of the apartment, shutting the door behind him. "It is. Though I can't see a reason to tell her of your unannounced visit." She hadn't once mentioned the male since he reappeared in her life. And he had no intention of leaving her alone ever again.

The male folded his arms across his chest. "That seems a little presumptuous of you. How do you know she didn't ask me over?"

Hamilton snickered. Was the overt muscle flex supposed to scare him? If that was the idiot's intention, it backfired. Big time. Just because they stood around the same height and had a similar build, he'd easily wipe the floor with this guy. "Because she has me. And she'd never settle for a pawn when she has a king."

"A king?" the male scoffed and uncrossed his arms. "I see nothing more than an errant prince who's desperately trying to fill his daddy's britches." With each word, the guy closed the distance between the two of them until they stood almost nose-to-nose. "Odessa will eventually see you for what you are. And when she does, she'll leave."

His jaw clenched as he balled up his fists. This mouthpiece had a lot of fucking nerve. Not that he could say which pissed him off more. The comments about his father…or Odessa. Either way, he needed to teach this scammer a lesson. Hamilton grabbed the guy by the throat and slammed him up against the wall. "I suggest you heed my warning and don't return. Odessa doesn't need you. Stay away."

The guy slapped his hand, which only made him squeeze harder. "Let go!" the mouthpiece choked out, gasping for air.

"Hamilton!" Odessa screamed. "What are you doing? Let him go!"

Shit, he thought to himself. He'd gotten so caught up with this pathetic excuse for a human, he hadn't noticed her get off the elevator. No matter. He'd made his point. Hamilton released the blond male, who crumpled into a heap against the wall as he struggled to catch his breath.

Odessa rushed over to the mouthpiece's side. "Oh my God, Austin. I'm so sorry. Are you okay?"

"He's fine," Hamilton muttered. He took a slight step back, but didn't go too far. As much as the guy deserved what happened, the last thing he ever wanted was for Odessa to see him like that.

Her gaze narrowed at Hamilton. "I didn't ask you," she snapped. She turned her attention back to Austin.

"I'm okay." The male's voice sounded hoarse as he pressed his hands against his knees. "Promise."

"See." Hamilton gestured toward the piece of shit. "Just like I said."

Odessa's jaw tightened. Glaring at him, she pointed at the door. "Go inside."

"Absolutely not. I'm not leaving you out here with…*him*." Had she fucking lost her mind? Didn't she see the twinkle in the scammer's eyes? Or how he milked the attention she gave him? No way was she this deluded to the surrounding danger.

"Excuse me." Jerking her head in his direction, she pursed her lips. Her muscles tensed as she drew herself up to her full height. "I suggest you wise the fuck up real fast. He's not the one I don't trust right now."

Hamilton opened his mouth and snapped it shut. Nope. The situation was bad enough. If he kept talking, he'd only make it worse. She hadn't seen how the male goaded him. Not that he should've played into it, but he couldn't change that now. With a slight snort, he gripped the back of his neck. "Fine. But if you're not inside in the next five minutes, then I'm coming back out here and dragging you in." Yeah, because *that* would make it better. Before he could stoop lower, Hamilton stormed to the front door of her apartment and disappeared inside.

He glanced down at the kitten, who tilted its head at him. It meowed.

"You should've stopped me," he grumbled. Sure. The kitten could've kept him from opening the door. Hamilton dragged a hand down his face and hung his head. What was wrong with him? He never acted like this. Or was this one of the wonderful side effects of his newfound vampirism that he hadn't noticed before? His ears twitched as he focused on the conversation on the other side of the door.

"There's some redness around your throat. God, I'm so sorry. Can I get you an ice pack or something?" Odessa offered.

"No, I'm alright. I just want to make sure you're going to be okay with *that* guy. I mean, who is he? Aside from someone you know," Austin replied.

"He's…a friend. It's sweet of you to worry, but he'd never hurt me."

A friend? Was that what she'd resigned him to? *A friend?* Obviously, they still had a lot to figure out, but friends didn't kiss. Not like they had. Nor did they argue the way they had. "Friends," Hamilton scoffed. "My ass."

"Are you positive it'll be safe? I'd hate for something to happen to you."

"Yes, Austin. I'll be fine," Odessa said. "Again, I'm so sorry for this. If you'll excuse me, I'm going to head inside."

Shit. Hamilton picked up Bard, who'd started rubbing against his leg. At least someone liked him at the moment. He rushed into the living room and plopped on the couch as silently as possible.

The front door opened, Odessa crossed the threshold, and shut the door behind her. She glared at him. "What are you doing here? No, better yet. How the hell did you get into my apartment?"

Seemed like an odd question. Unless she hadn't figured out how he'd gotten in the last few times he'd shown up. "Through the window in your bedroom. You really should lock that."

"I did!" Spinning on the back of her heel, she stomped down the hallway.

"Wait, what?" He jumped to his feet, trailing after her. "I'm telling you, Dess, it was unlocked." Given the current climate, this wasn't something either of them could overlook. Though his uncle had never used family in the past, he wouldn't put it past the male to stoop to this level. Odessa wasn't quite *family*. Even if they'd gotten married, it wouldn't matter to Claude. Not with what he believed his uncle had done to his father.

"And somehow that gives you permission to break into my apartment? This isn't our shared space, Hamilton." Odessa stormed into her bedroom and crossed the room to the window. Staring at it, she flipped the lever and shook her head. "This isn't possible. Maintenance just fixed this a week ago."

Hamilton frowned. Nothing she said sounded good. While his uncle would purposely break a lock, Odessa would've recognized him as maintenance. Still, something about it bothered him. "What are you talking about? Why would they have needed to come in?"

"I found the lock on the front window and this one shaved down. It's how I ended up with Bard. He snuck in through the window. But I know they were both fixed. I watched maintenance make the repairs." Odessa faced him. Her gaze flicked to the kitten in his arms.

"You're joking, right?" He cocked an eyebrow at her. Although the stern look in her eyes softened, she shrugged. "Hunters can't take an animal form. Only shapeshifters can do that. Well, and some witches and demons. But none of them have ever taken the form of a common house cat." At least not that he'd seen or read about. Not that he offered her that tidbit. It seemed pointless. Bard was not his uncle in animal form. "Someone more than likely broke into your apartment and sabotaged the locking mechanism. All the more reason for you to come stay with me."

"We're not having this conversation again." She inhaled and exhaled a deep breath. "I'll just have maintenance come back out tomorrow. Maybe have them change the whole window or use a different locking system."

"Do you think that's going to stop him?" Hamilton scoffed. "Claude is a hunter. Not an ordinary human. If he wants to break into your apartment and break the lock, then he'll do it." That didn't mean he couldn't keep her safe. He just had to be smart about his actions. They both did. Surveying the bedroom, his eyes landed on the wooden bat sitting in her closet. It wasn't much, but in a pinch, it would do. He set the kitten on the floor, strode across the bedroom, and retrieved the bat.

"If my life is in such danger, then what do you think that'll do? Or do you plan to beat him to death with it?"

"No." Though he could smell the fear rolling off of her, it wasn't nearly enough. As much as he wanted her to understand the danger, he wouldn't tell her just how bad it truly was. He crossed the room, stopped in front of the window, and jammed the bat across the top pane. No one would open it from the outside again. Hamilton peered over his shoulder at her and pointed at the bat. "This only comes out when you let me in. Got it?"

Odessa wrapped her arms around herself. "You could always just use the front door like a normal person."

"Except I want to find Claude before he finds me. Going through the front leaves a trail. One that another can easily follow." Especially if they searched for him. And this only reaffirmed his suspicion.

"What if you don't?" She gestured to the bat. "I can't stay here like a prisoner. That's not any better than forcing me to live with you."

"That's not my intention." Hamilton closed the distance between them. He enveloped her in his arms. "Keeping you safe doesn't mean you can't live your life, Dess. It just means…I'll be here with you. Night and day, as long as you're here."

Her arms came around his waist, gripping him tightly. "Promise?"

Slipping his finger beneath her chin, he lifted her face until their gazes met. "You're all that matters to me. That has been true since the day we met. And it will remain so until the day I die."

The corners of her mouth lifted into a lopsided smile. "Some days, Hamilton…Morck, I swear you know just the right thing to say." Odessa pushed up on her tiptoes and fused her lips to his, coaxing his mouth open. Their tongues entwined, deepening the kiss.

Despite the anger she'd expressed mere moments ago, her scent flared in his nostrils. Fuck. He'd never turned her on so easily before. At least, not in a way that flipped her switch from anger to lust so quickly. Though he tried, he couldn't deny the need to touch her. Hamilton caressed the nape of her neck, gingerly running his fingers up and down.

A soft moan escaped her mouth as she tilted her head back, leaning into the palm of his hand. Their eyes locked on one another. "Don't stop," she whispered.

The last couple of times they kissed, he'd done just that. But he wasn't strong enough to do it again, especially with the way her bright-green eyes sparkled. Hamilton captured her mouth and slid his hands further down her back. He groaned into the kiss as he deepened it more.

Without breaking the kiss, Odessa yanked on his tie's knot, nearly tearing it as she undid it with a quickness. She tossed it over her shoulder, where it landed somewhere on the floor. The two of them worked together in a comingled mess of hands to remove his jacket and button-down and her coat and blouse.

Gripping her ass, he lifted her up. Her legs wrapped around his waist. The warmth from that juncture between her legs rolled off of her in waves, hardening his cock. God, he needed to bury himself inside of her like there was no tomorrow.

Their tongues tangled in a ferocious battle. She reached down, unzipped her boots one at a time, and kicked each one off. Her fingers curled around the back of his neck. As he carried her over to the bed, he trailed one hand up her spine. Heat blazed through his veins, lighting his synapses on fire. Not that it felt like enough. No matter how much of her he felt in his hands, he yearned for more.

Hamilton unhooked her bra and slipped one strap over her shoulder as he broke off the kiss. Lowering her to the bed, he traced kisses along her jawline and hovered over her. Their gazes met as everything around them fell silent. He drank in the sight of her swollen lips, the way her chest rose and fell with each ragged breath she took, and the sheen in her bright-green eyes. "Stunning."

Without giving her a chance to respond, he locked his lips with hers in an unhurried, sensual kiss. As much as he longed to feel every part of her, he also wanted to take his time. Being without her this last year had nearly taken its toll on him. Only the hope of reuniting with her one day kept him going. Though it hadn't happened in the way he always dreamed, now that he had her, he wouldn't let her go. Lazily stroking his fingers across her shoulders, he tugged the bra straps down, removed it, and threw it to the side.

Odessa moaned. She ran her hands down his biceps and forearms. Arching her back, she pressed her breasts against his chest.

The skin-to-skin contact sent a blaze of heat right to his cock, thickening his erection. Fuck, he needed to feel all of her. Hamilton kicked off his shoes, flinging them across the floor, as he gripped her ass and ground his shaft against the juncture between her legs. A groan left them both simultaneously.

She hooked her legs over his ass cheeks, tightening her hold on him. Not that he minded in the least. It only got him harder and intensified his need for her. Odessa dragged her nails up his back, marking him as hers.

Hamilton brushed his thumb across her nipple as he kneaded her breast. He broke off the kiss, ran his fingertips up her side, and trailed a path to the valley between her breasts. A low rumble sounded in his chest. Fuck, she fit so perfectly in the palm of his hand. He latched onto her nipple, stroking his tongue across it with a deep, guttural moan.

"Oh, God!" she cried out, digging her nails harder into his back.

An uncontrollable need to get inside of her blazed through him. He snapped the button on her jeans, yanked the sides apart, nearly ripping the material as he tore them down her legs. His own pants barely fared much better. Not that it mattered. All that mattered was that hardly a stitch of clothing remained between them.

Hamilton stood there and drank in every inch of her gorgeous body. He skimmed his fingers up her long legs, mesmerized by each nuance of her alabaster skin. Though he'd never forgotten how she looked in a moment of pure ecstasy, with that glossy look in her green eyes, it was like seeing her for the first time all over again. And they'd only just started. Hooking his thumbs into the edges of her black lace underwear, he stripped them from her body and tossed them aside.

Slowly, he crawled up onto the bed and hovered over her. Slipping his fingers into her folds, he thrust in and out as he reclaimed her lips. Wrapping her legs around his waist, Odessa lifted her hips and rocked her sex against his digits. Fuck, she was so wet. His shaft throbbed. As much as he wanted to taste her, he couldn't wait any longer. Though he'd absolutely have his fill of her before the night was over.

He removed his fingers from her sex, brought them to his mouth, and licked off all of her juices. Without taking a breath, Hamilton pressed the blunt head of his cock to her entrance. Fusing their lips together, their tongues engaged in an epic battle. He pulled his hips back and thrust deeper inside of her sex.

They moaned. He couldn't quite tell where either of their noises ended or began. By the end of the night, they'd create a whole symphony of their own design. Odessa gripped the bedding above her head. Except that wasn't what he wanted. Nor was it what he needed. He moved one of her hands to his shoulder and grasped the other, entwining their fingers together as he brought his hips back once again. This time, he slid all the way home; her sex fully sheathing his shaft.

Holy fuck. She felt even more amazing than he remembered, especially as her nails dug into his shoulder. The slight pinpricks sent a new set of jolts racing across his synapses. Hamilton wrapped an arm around her waist and gripped the small of her back as he pistoned in and out of her sex.

Odessa pressed her feet against his ass and lifted her hips, meeting each of his thrusts. Her back arched, pressing her breasts against his chest. "Oh, God," she groaned. "Don't stop."

No chance of that happening. Not that he responded verbally. He readjusted his position, bracing his knees more against her thighs, and increased his pace. Fuck. At this rate, he didn't imagine it would take either of them long to come. It would only be the first of many orgasms of the night. He planned to ensure they were both fully satisfied before sleep claimed either of them.

The walls of her sex clenched around his shaft, sending shivers down his spine. "Fuck!" Hamilton swung his hips faster and slammed into her sex like a wild animal. The grip she had on his hand tightened. Though the prick of pain barely registered. His fangs extended with a slight hiss. He buried his face into the crook of her neck and grazed her throat with his fangs as he pulled her body flush against his. The slightly altered angle allowed him to penetrate her deeper and harder.

That was all it took to push them both over the edge. Odessa cried out his name as an orgasm exploded out of her body, completely drenching his shaft. A powerful release shot up the length of his cock, filling her up. He didn't stop until their mutual orgasms reached their end. "Holy shit," Hamilton mumbled.

Through ragged breaths, he brushed a soft kiss across her shoulder, lifted his head, and swept her hair aside. His gaze fell over her face. "Are you okay?" It wasn't something he would've normally asked, but something had changed in him in those last moments. Not that he could identify what. Maybe he should dig into it before they continued, except his desire to have her again consumed every part of his body. It wasn't something he could deny himself.

Odessa lit up. "I'm perfect."

"Good." He grinned widely. "I was worried I might've hurt you."

"Not at all."

"I'm glad to hear that." Hamilton pressed a tender kiss to her lips and caressed her jawline with his fangs. "We're just getting started and I definitely don't want you sore." The gasp that left Odessa's mouth told him everything he needed to know. They'd both enjoy what came next.

eleven

"ARE YOU SURE ABOUT THIS?" Odessa asked. The suggestion he'd made last night as they laid entangled in one another's arms still didn't make a lick of sense to her. How could his mother confirm his uncle's whereabouts? Why would the woman even wish him dead? What kind of mother did that? Did the change from hunter to vampire really matter that much?

"Dess, you started the book I gave you earlier. You know the answer to that."

"I just wish there was another way." She didn't want to dredge up terrible memories for Gladys. No one else understood the pain she'd gone through losing him. Something that still lingered, even though he stood here in front of her. Everything about the last few days seemed so surreal, especially last night.

Hamilton sat beside her on the couch and draped an arm across her shoulders, tucking her into his side. "I know. But this is the best way. It keeps you out of the cross-hairs. I'd never forgive myself if something happened to you."

She pressed a soft kiss to the bottom of his jaw. "I don't want anything to happen to you, either. I just got you back." If she lost him again, she'd never pick up the pieces. Not that she said as much.

"You won't. I promise." Hamilton brushed his lips across hers. "Please make the call."

"If you're sure this will work, I'll do it." Not that they had much in the way of choices. They'd spent the better part of the morning calling around motels in the city, where he suspected Claude might stay. That had gotten them nowhere. There were too many places to check. At least this way, they brought Claude to them. Or so she hoped.

"It will. Hunters are sworn to protect human life. It won't matter that I'm her son."

Odessa shook her head in disgust. Something that still didn't sound right. Though every entry she'd read in the book he'd given her indicated the same thing. Species mattered more than blood. It practically granted permission to even kill children if they were vampiric or shapeshifter kids. Nothing could make her wrap her head around that. "Alright. I'll call."

"Good." With a slight nod, he removed his arm from around her and ran his fingers across the top of Bard's head.

Her kitten had taken a liking to Hamilton's lap. Not that she could blame him. Inhaling and exhaling a deep breath, Odessa picked up her cell phone and selected his mother's number from her contact list. They hadn't spoken since before her move to New York. That should prevent things from being strange. The line rang twice.

"Hello?" Hamilton's mother answered.

"Gladys, hi. It's me, Odessa." She fidgeted with the hem of her silk blouse. "I hope I'm not catching you at a bad time."

"Not at all. How are you doing, Odessa? Everything go okay with the move?"

"For the most part." She paused. It was more for dramatic effect than anything else. Flicking her gaze to Hamilton, she reminded herself of his idea the night before. *All you have to do is tell her my ghost is haunting you.* Not that she'd use those exact words, but it had given her a direction. "I mean, I got settled in okay, but that's not why I'm calling."

"Oh?" Concern registered in Gladys's voice. "What's going on, Odessa? You know you can talk to me about anything. Right?"

"Of course." That used to be the case. Now, she no longer believed that. Odessa let out a heavy sigh. "I've been…seeing things. Like how I used to…I thought…I thought I'd left it behind, but it seems to have followed me."

"Have you spoken to Dr. Carmichael about this? Or your father?"

"No." For such a simple answer, it had so many factors behind it. She glanced at Hamilton out of her periphery. This was the only possible way to get Claude here. With how personal she had to get, she hoped it worked. Then they could get on with their lives. But having him so close… Odessa angled her body a bit, turning away from Hamilton. "I'm afraid if I did, they'd…commit me…" her words trailed off. She couldn't say that part. Not that she had to, Gladys was well aware of it. "I'm not losing my mind…I just…I need you to remind me of what we saw. Of *that* day."

"Oh, honey."

"I'm sorry to ask this of you, Gladys, but I just…I can't go on like this. It's like I'm cursed to see him everywhere I look. My job…home…I didn't think anyone else would understand." They shared a pain like no other. Yes, she'd gotten him back, but nothing would ever change the agony that had struck her the day Hamilton died.

A loud knock sounded at the door. Odessa peered over her shoulder from the couch. She shut off the television and eyed the time on her watch. Three in the morning. It had to be Hamilton. He'd stormed out earlier after their argument and hadn't returned home yet. Which was why she hadn't gotten a wink of sleep, no matter how much she'd tried. She got to her feet and strode toward the door. "Did you forget your key again?"

Another rap on the door, followed by the doorbell, echoed around the apartment.

"Impatient much," Odessa muttered. He was the idiot who'd locked himself out. If she didn't love him so much, she'd leave him outside until morning. He

deserved nothing less for the way he'd acted. She opened the door and blinked. Instead of her fiancé stood two police officers. "Um, can I help you?"

"I'm Sergeant Bernardo and this is Officer Osric. Are you Odessa Black?"

"Yes, I am." The grip she had on the door tightened. Her face blanched. She swallowed saliva to wet her parched throat. The police didn't just show up on people's doorsteps at this time of morning for no reason. Oh, God. No, no, no. "Why are you here? Is my father okay? My brother? Hamilton?"

"Miss Black, may we please come inside?"

Something had happened. Of that much, she was sure, but neither of these men gave anything away. They just gave one another a small glance. One of them had an answer. Why wouldn't they just tell her? "No!" Odessa screamed. Tears welled in the corners of her eyes. "Tell me right now! What is it? Who's hurt?"

"I'm sorry, Miss Black. We found the body of Hamilton Kring earlier this morning."

"No," she choked out on a sob. Her grip on the doorframe loosened and she stumbled back a few steps. She couldn't have heard him right. "He was fine," Odessa mumbled. Hamilton had only left five hours ago. The officer had to be wrong. The love of her life wasn't gone. He wasn't. Her chest constricted and her vision blurred. This wasn't happening. It wasn't. "I can't breathe." The world around her spun. Her heart pounded inside her chest as her knees gave out.

One officer had caught her before she collapsed. Not that she recalled which one. Nor did it matter. That news had completely devastated her. Odessa reached over and squeezed Hamilton's leg. He was here with her and alive in his own way.

"It's just your heart playing tricks on you, Odessa. The Hamilton we loved…he's gone. You know this," Gladys said.

God, she'd nearly forgotten she was on the phone with the woman. Her mind had gone off while the female spoke. Not that Gladys seemed to notice. With a sniffle, Odessa brushed the tears from her cheeks. "You're right. Thank you, Gladys."

"Odessa, I'm always happy to help." The woman paused. "You know what, Claude is out there on business. Since you don't want to involve your father, why don't I ask him to check on you? Make sure there aren't any more random appearances of Hamilton."

"Thank you, Gladys. That would be lovely." Yeah, that worked out great. Just as she and Hamilton hoped it would. She glanced at him and dipped her chin, confirming his suspicions.

"Of course. Now, go get some rest. You sound as if you could use it."

"I will. Have a good evening." The pleasantry at the end nauseated her. It made the conversation seem so normal, though it was anything but that. A woman she once respected had just shown her true colors. How could Gladys throw Hamilton away like a common piece of trash?

"You as well, Odessa."

With that, she disconnected the line. Her eyes fell to the screen as it darkened, ending the call as if it had never happened. Odessa wiped the last of her tears from her face and set her cell phone on the table. "You were right. Claude is here in New York."

Hamilton set Bard on the floor, gently gripped Odessa's chin, and lifted her gaze to meet his. "Are you alright? That didn't sound like an easy phone call."

"I'm okay. I just…I remembered when the police showed up on our front door step." The words that had left the officer's mouth…she'd always known how powerful words could be, but in that moment, they'd broken her in a way she hadn't known existed. And she'd lost her mother at a young age, yet the agony of each differed. Back then, all she'd thought about was the last things they said to one another. Now she realized it went beyond that. She'd lost the one person in this world who truly understood her.

"I'm sorry you had to go through that. Not just back then, but that you had to relive that moment. I never wanted that."

"I know. But I'm glad I remembered it." She covered his hand with her own and pressed a kiss to his palm. "It reminded me why we're doing this. I mean…things may not be ideal, but we have each other." Their eyes met. "And I won't let anyone take that away from us again. Not even your uncle."

The corners of his lips lifted into a broad grin. "Just when I think I couldn't love you more, Odessa Black, you prove me wrong." Hamilton brushed a tender kiss across her lips. "What do you say we get out of here? Get some food?"

"That sounds like a marvelous idea. But don't you think someone might notice us leaving?" He'd suggested someone watched her apartment for Claude. Or the male had taken up residence nearby and did it himself. Either way, it made sense for her to stay put.

"Not the way I plan for us to leave." He stood, pulling her up with him.

Odessa's eyebrows furrowed. "If we don't go out the door, how else would we…?" Her eyes widened. He hadn't used the front door once since he showed up in her apartment the first time. "Oh, no! Absolutely not!"

"Come on, Dess. It's perfectly safe."

"From where? The roof?" They were on the fifth floor. It wasn't a skyscraper, but jumping from this height would break bones. Climbing up was the only way out, provided they didn't use the door.

"Well, we can travel that way if you prefer, but I figured down was more appropriate. You're already dressed. Though if you intend to bring your phone, I'd recommend tucking it away in your back pocket." Hamilton wrapped his arms around her and kissed her forehead. "Hey. I promise you; this is safe. Trust me."

Of all the things he had to say, he had to use those words. Two tiny words that held so much meaning. Because she trusted him. Not just to protect her heart, but her body, too. Cracking a smile, Odessa shook her head, grabbed her cell phone, and tucked it into the back pocket of her jeans. "Then let's go."

"That's my girl." He marched down the hall, tugging her along behind him. They grabbed a coat for her out of the hall closet and headed to the bedroom. Once they reached the window in her bedroom, he removed the bat, set it aside, and got everything opened up to the balcony.

The two of them climbed out onto the metal framework and shut the window. She eyed the brick building across from them. Her gaze fell to the alleyway below. From this height, she could make out a few scattered cardboard boxes, a couple of crows picking at something, and a dumpster at the other end of the alley. Oh, this was a bad idea. "Holy shit," she grumbled. Her heart raced. The hairs on the back of her neck stood at attention. A shiver shot down her spine. She squeezed her eyes shut tight. "Oh, God. I can't do this."

"Hey. Yes, you can. Just focus on me and grab on tight," Hamilton instructed. "I'll handle the rest."

Right. Inhaling and exhaling a deep breath, Odessa lifted her gaze to him, hugged her arms around his neck, and laced her fingers together. Situating his arm around her waist, he pulled her flush against his body. Warmth spread through her chest. Though the breeze bristled across her cheek, everything around them disappeared.

"Good girl."

She barely noticed him push off the balcony. Not until a gust of wind ruffled her coat and blouse. Seconds later, they landed on the ground and a flock of birds took off all around them. Her eyes widened as she drank in their surroundings. Everything she'd seen from above, except it wasn't all so small. She could even smell the mixed stench of rotting garbage and stale cigarettes a lot better. Odessa glimpsed her balcony several stories above them. She chuckled. "That is definitely the easier way to travel."

"And now you know exactly how I get in and out of your apartment." He brushed a soft kiss across her lips, draped an arm across her shoulders, and hugged her tight against his side. "Now, let's go get food."

"I still think you should use the door." His groan didn't impress her. Though it made her laugh. Something they could talk more about over dinner.

Hamilton threaded his fingers with Odessa's as they strolled through the park. He adjusted their direction, turning them toward Temperance Fountain. Their steps crunched the fallen leaves carpeting the walkway. A beautiful array of bold red, sunshine yellow, and fiery orange. One of the many things he enjoyed about this park. And one of the few he could enjoy a leisurely walk with his fiancée after a wonderful dinner. "This place is gorgeous this time of year."

"I think everywhere I've seen of New York is like that." Odessa offered him a warm smile and rested her head against his pec.

"It is certainly a stunning city. Though you need to be careful where you travel, especially at night." Some places were completely off-limits. He'd have to put a list together for her. Something he could take care of later.

"What do you mean?" Snuggling closer, Odessa wrapped a hand around his biceps.

"Shapeshifters, hunters, and witches roam the city. While some areas aren't under anyone's control, they have claimed others. For example, the shapeshifters have control of Washington State Park. We avoid that place." It wasn't the only park shapeshifters ruled. Thankfully, this one was neutral territory. The likelihood they'd run into any of the other species was slim. Although he couldn't avoid every fight, he preferred to prevent whatever was in his power.

"Do you really think it's necessary? I mean, for me? Even alone?"

Hamilton cracked a bemused smile. "Normally, I'd say no, except…," he leaned in close, pressed his nose to her hair, and took a big whiff, "you kind of smell like me."

"I do not!" she protested and playfully swatted his chest.

"Hey, I'm not saying you stink. Just that you carry my scent on you." He'd made damn certain she had it all over her last night. If he had his way, he'd absolutely do it again tonight. That just depended on how long things took with Claude. "I'm being serious, Dess. Witches may not have enhanced smell, but shapeshifters and hunters do. They could use you to get to me. To kill me."

"Then I'll stay away from whatever places you tell me." Odessa lifted her head off his shoulder. "Hamilton? How did Claude…?" She bit her bottom lip. "How did it happen?"

Right. It made sense she wanted to know. The police hadn't ever solved his case. Not that they would've figured it out. Unless they had someone with knowledge of the supernatural in their precinct. He glimpsed at her out of his periphery. Determination sparkled in her green eyes. No way could he deny her the truth. After all she'd endured, she deserved to know more than what he'd already shared. "Claude and I had been hunting this witch. We'd stumbled onto one of their kills a few weeks earlier."

Hamilton peered at her. He paused long enough to give her a chance to ask for details. That wasn't something she really needed running amok in her head. When she merely nodded at him, he continued, "My uncle messaged me, told me he'd located the witch we were after. I didn't realize it was a trap."

"How could you notice something like that? I mean, before it happened. Even with the type of person Claude is, I can't see how you could've anticipated his actions."

"Do you recall when my father died the year before? How it had come out of nowhere?" A sudden death he'd later learned occurred from poison. One that no one could detect beyond the first twenty-four hours after death. There was only one thing he still didn't know. Whether his mother was involved. Hamilton caught Odessa's acknowledgment. "While Claude and I were searching for that witch, I was investigating my father's death. I'd come to believe Claude killed him."

"What? Why would he do that?"

Hamilton shrugged. "I have my suspicions, but I wasn't ever able to confirm it."

"What do you think?"

"Our family is a legacy family regarding hunters. My father lived up to that which our ancestors created, as did I. Claude never quite measured up. I think that finally caught up to him. That he did something that would've resulted in my father stripping him of his title and powers." It didn't happen often. He'd only witnessed it once in his life. A stripped hunter went through a horrific change in front of those who shunned them. Not an image he wanted in Odessa's head.

"So…you think Claude killed your father to stop that?"

"Yes. My mother may have been complacent about it or used Claude afterward for her own gain. I'm not sure. Either is possible. But that's not the point of all this." He had to get back to the topic at hand. She wanted to know about his death. "Claude and I agreed to meet at a warehouse where he'd supposedly tracked the witch. I went in first. By the time I realized the place was empty, it was too late. Although I'm a capable fighter, his trap put me in a weakened state. Made it easier for Claude to physically overpower me."

"I can't imagine what that must've been like," Odessa commented as they approached the side of Temperance Fountain.

"It's not something I think much about these days. You are." That was the utter truth. He hadn't wished to shed his vampiric nature for his family. It was only so he could return to her. Though, she seemed to accept him as he was now. Maybe he could learn to do the same with time. Hamilton pressed a kiss to her forehead and squeezed her hand.

"If you're trying to get lucky tonight, you're doing a good job." She pushed up on her tiptoes and fused their lips together.

Something rustled nearby and the hairs on the nape of his neck stood at attention. Hamilton broke off the kiss and scanned their surroundings. He surveyed the trees beyond the four supporting columns they stood by. A few squirrels leaped from branch to branch. The slaps of a jogger's footsteps sounded on the other side of the park. Another couple chit-chatted together, but from their position, they came from Avenue B. Nothing appeared out of the ordinary.

The whistle of a swinging pipe jerked his head to Odessa. He lifted a hand and caught the piece of metal aimed at hitting her. As his palm burned, he flipped his gaze to the male holding the other end of the pipe.

Shit. A hunter. "Run!" Hamilton hollered as he jumped in front of her.

Odessa took a few steps back, turned, and ran. The sound of her boots pounding against the pavement eased his worry. At least a little.

He yanked on the silver-coated pipe. Despite the way it seared his flesh, he needed it far away before he took on this hunter. Not that the male seemed too eager to let it go. Then again, maybe he didn't have to hold on to it to get it out of the way. Grabbing onto the cylindrical weapon with his other hand, he shoved it backward and stabbed the guy in the shoulder.

The hunter grunted, wrenched the pipe free from his body, and tossed it aside. He pulled a machete from his back and pointed it at Hamilton. "I'm going to enjoy this."

Another blade. Also likely coated in silver or possibly made from it. One of a few things that could actually hurt him. He definitely had to be careful in his movement. But he couldn't take it easy on this guy, either. Hamilton extended his claws and fangs. With a growl, he charged at the hunter.

The guy parried and swung the machete at him from overhead, which he just dodged. Hamilton swiped his claws at the hunter, catching him across the face. Blood freckled the guy's cheek as he stumbled backward.

Nothing about how this guy moved appeared familiar. Usually, he recognized something about their training. But he couldn't pinpoint anything. Somewhere behind him, Odessa screamed. Hamilton looked toward the noise. Another hunter had gone after his fiancée.

He hissed at the pain that radiated up his arm. Hamilton refocused his attention on the male in front of him. The guy had taken advantage of his moment of distraction and sliced him with the blade. As expected, someone had coated it in silver. A low rumble resounded in his chest. Hamilton darted around the skinny-ass hunter, stopped behind him, and grabbed onto each side of his head. "I'm going to enjoy this," he repeated the male's words back and then snapped his neck.

The hunter crumpled into a heap of flesh and bones with a resounding thud, and the machete skittered across the ground. Now to deal with the one that had gone after Odessa. Hamilton stalked around the stone kiosk, raced across the square, and leaped into the air. He landed on the back of the other hunter. Without hesitation, he latched onto the male's throat, bit down, and tore it out.

As the second body collapsed to the turf, he ran over to Odessa's side. Hamilton wiped the blood from his mouth and crouched down next to her. The only visible wounds he spotted were a stitch of crimson and a cut across her forehead. She'd gotten knocked out again. Her heart beat strong, though, so it didn't sound as if he had much to worry about. Still, he needed to get them out of here, and fast. This wasn't a mess that humans needed to stumble upon.

Hamilton dug his cell phone out of his pocket and called the only person who could handle the situation. The butler answered on the first ring. "Grayson, I need a pick up and clean up. Tompkins Square Park, pronto."

"Yes, sir." The line disconnected.

Lack of questions. Just the way he liked it. He tucked the phone in the inside pocket of his jacket, slid his arms under Odessa, and scooped her up. "Don't worry, Dess. I got you."

Twelve

ODESSA STIRRED AWAKE. HER HEAD throbbed. How was that even possible? She didn't recall…oh, right. Someone attacked her and Hamilton in the park. Well, a couple of people. One male knocked her down, and she hit her forehead on the sidewalk. Why did they always go for the head? Crikey!

It took a moment for her eyes to focus. What the hell? Where was she? Odessa bolted upright. With a groan, she gripped her forehead. Shit. Bad idea. That only worsened the stabbing pain. She blew out a breath and curled her fingers against the velvet duvet as it slowly eased to a mild ache.

She surveyed the bedroom because it definitely didn't belong to her. Someone had laid her down in a four-poster king-sized bed with a crushed-red-velvet cover. Not something she would've chosen herself. A golden swirling pattern coated the walls. God, that looked like it could make someone dizzy. Unless she was seeing things resulting from her head injury. Which made some sense, except for the statues scattered around the room.

This place looked more like a museum than a place to rest. Either way, she refused to stay put. Odessa got to her feet. At least she still had her boots on; something she didn't have to find if she had to run. With a quick scan of the room, she located the door and made her way toward it.

Odessa paused in front of a round mirror to the right of the door. What in the world? She lifted her fingers to her forehead and tenderly touched the stitched-up cut. It was where she'd hit her head. Who would take the time to…? She peered over her shoulder, surveying the landscape of the room again. Could she be in Hamilton's bedroom? They'd never discussed where he lived or the details of his current life. Given the attire she'd seen him in lately, it made sense that this was his place.

A brief memory flickered in the back of her mind. She'd come around earlier. And she'd seen a splash of blood across Hamilton's…his face and arm. Something had looked off about it, not that she could surmise what. Even now, the information eluded her. Gripping the back of her neck, she stared at her reflection in the mirror. God, she had so many questions about what happened.

She'd get them answered…once she found Hamilton. If this was his place, he had to be around somewhere. He wouldn't just leave her alone like this. Odessa gripped the doorknob and gently eased it open. Without confirmation of her location, it served her best to act as if danger lurked around every corner.

Slipping out of the bedroom into a carpeted hallway, she pressed her back close to the wall. Her eyes gravitated across the various paintings hung along each side of the hall. Picasso. Da Vinci. Those were just among the ones she recognized. Most of them she couldn't identify the artist or the work. Though the consistent imagery of angels, including more statues, disturbed her a little. No way this place belonged to a vampire.

Refocusing on her task, Odessa checked both directions and spotted a staircase not too far off. She headed toward it, lingering for a moment to eye the waterfall painted on the wall beside it. Voices echoed from somewhere down below. Maybe one floor below her. A soft breath escaped her as one of them sounded familiar—Hamilton.

Oh, thank God, she thought to herself. Not only was he alive, but this had to be his home. As she descended the staircase, she listened intently to the conversation.

"That's when I called Grayson," Hamilton said. "Time was of the essence, and it was the best call I could've made."

"I believe you," the male paused. "I'm curious. Do you feel any remorse for taking the lives of those young hunters?"

"They endangered Odessa's life. What do you think?"

Odessa stopped halfway down the stairs at Hamilton's words. *Oh, God!* He'd killed them. Although she'd seen the blood on his face, what it meant hadn't truly registered. He'd told her to run, and she'd done just that. Left him to handle the mess. Why should this surprise her? Hamilton had planned to kill Claude. He'd made that abundantly clear. No reason he'd react differently to other hunters. What made her life more important than theirs? Or did he simply have so little disregard for the lives of others?

"Hmph," the male responded.

"What does that mean? Oh, no! Whatever idea is tumbling around in that head of yours, the answer is no."

"Hamilton, you have an opportunity here. You cannot pass upon it because it doesn't suit your desires."

"Yes, I can. Especially if it's what I think you're thinking."

"Which is what?" the male snorted derisively. "Because last I checked, you don't possess the power of telepathy."

"That two different factions have now used Odessa to get to me. Possibly even one. Meaning it would benefit us to use her as bait. Maybe brusque, but how'd I do?" Hamilton scoffed. "Don't worry. The look on your face answers that."

Right. *He* valued her life above all others. They loved one another. But that didn't make his assessment right. Nor did she fully agree with the other male. Not entirely, anyway. Odessa continued her descent to the first floor.

"Yes, I believe it would benefit us to use her presence to our advantage. Or have you forgotten what remains at stake?"

"Of course not!" Hamilton retorted. "But I will not purposely put her in the path of danger."

"Except you already have. Though, perhaps we should allow her to decide. It is her life, after all."

"Absolutely not, Theo. I've decided for both of us. End of discussion."

Odessa hit the bottom of the staircase and stopped. *Oh, hell no.* They'd talked about this. He'd tell her everything. And she'd bet her life savings that he didn't intend to mention any of what she'd overheard. Her gaze flicked in the direction the voices had come from; a study if she had to guess. At least from what she saw through the cracked door. She strolled across the marble floor, heading right for them.

"If you are certain."

The study door opened further. A dark-haired male with a widow's peak and piercing, blue eyes stood in the doorway. Odessa stopped just on the other side. *Holy shit.* It looked as if the painting she'd seen in that book had come to life. The family tree. All of those males named Theodore. It all made sense. "Theodore Morck, I take it," she said.

"At your service, Miss Black." He bowed to her, sweeping his hand out with a grand flourish.

"I'd say it's a pleasure, but I imagine the circumstances could be quite different." And she wouldn't feel so underdressed in a blouse and jeans compared to his five-piece dark-blue suit. That much she could identify. Her gaze flicked to Hamilton, who stood there with his mouth agape. She folded her arms across her chest. "For the record, I agree with Theodore."

Hamilton stalked out of the study and caressed her arms. "No, Dess. We don't need to stoop to their level."

Stoop? Was that how he saw it? Odessa smirked and glanced from Hamilton to Theo, then back again. "It wouldn't be. We'd pull them in to our level. You both seem to think these attacks are coming from multiple directions, but I believe you're overlooking the bigger picture. I think they're all stemming from one person—Claude."

"Interesting," Theodore commented as he clasped his hands behind him. "What makes you draw that conclusion?"

"Simple." Although she answered another's question, she focused her attention on Hamilton. This was too important for him not to see. "Claude suggested where I move. Possibly even where to work, but that's just a guess. The thugs…the first time…that's the night you told me the truth about you. Then tonight, less than a couple of hours after I speak with your mother, we're attacked again, except by hunters. It all points to Claude orchestrating all of it. With everything I know about him and what you've told me, it wouldn't surprise me if he's been watching us for days. Or even longer."

"Except Claude has never been that organized. Nor does it explain the vampire that followed you. Or how he'd even arrange that."

"Well, I can't explain the vampire. That doesn't really fit what I'm basing everything on, but think about the rest. Maybe his organizational skills lacked in the past, but he's also never had to kill someone twice." Or so she assumed. Everything she knew and learned over the last few days about Claude suggested one thing—he didn't intend to fail a second time.

Hamilton scoffed and dragged a hand down his face. "You have a point. I'm basically a unicorn for him. That alone…it would push any hunter to extremes." He brushed her cheek with the back of his knuckles. "I just don't want you to get hurt again."

"I know, but I won't stand by and do nothing. Nor will I run. I've done that enough, and it's getting us nowhere." They had to learn to work together. She glanced at Theodore, who still stood there, silently listening.

"Then what do you suggest?"

"He wants us to come out of the shadows, so that's what we'll do. We'll get seen around town, work together from the library to hunt for him afterward, and then train during the day." Her gaze shifted to Theodore. "I assume it's something you both do."

"Yes. You're quite welcome to join us. I think it'll be good…all around," he replied. "Don't you agree, Hamilton?"

"No, but I'm not positive my vote counts in this arena." Hamilton tucked a strand of Odessa's hair behind her ear. "Are you sure about this?"

"I am. I'm no one's pawn." And it was damn time she acted like it.

Hamilton held the greenhouse's glass door open for Odessa. He'd given her a full tour of the main part of the house, including the first and second story, and then led her out here. With their stroll through the park cut short, this seemed like the best alternative. He took her hand in his own, threading their fingers together as they walked along the cobblestone pathway. The chlorine from the nearby pool and hot tub comingled with the salty air assaulted his nostrils. This time of year wasn't good for swimming, but that didn't mean he couldn't show her an exquisite view of the ocean. "Aside from a few spots out here, that concludes the tour of the manor."

"It's beautiful. A little over the top with irony, but I'm guessing the décor is more Theodore's taste."

"Honestly, I'm not sure. He's always clammed up anytime I asked about the manor or its design." Not that he'd questioned it in quite some time. He'd only focused on the cure for the last several months. Maybe longer. "But I don't really see the irony."

Odessa raised an eyebrow. "Really? All the angels? And God imagery?" She gestured to the statue sitting on a grassy embankment near the pool. "Or *gods*, I guess I should say?"

"You haven't gotten to the creation of vampires in the book yet, have you?" He'd given her the book a couple of days ago. She'd often gotten through tomes he read faster than he did. Her eagerness to learn—one of many things he loved about her.

"No, but I haven't had a lot of time. And I told you, I'm not fluent in Aramaic. Which means I take longer to translate."

"Right," he responded as they strolled around the gazebo. Hamilton led Odessa toward the deck's edge, where they could lean against the metallic railing. "Vampires all come from Cain. He was the first of our existence."

"Oh." She stared out across the ocean. A comfortable silence stretched between them. Odessa turned a bit, angling her body toward his. "Is that why that pipe affected you earlier?"

"Well, yes. It wasn't just any regular pipe, though. The hunters coated it in silver. Same with the machete, the one faun pulled on me." And the guy had used it while he'd gotten distracted. Though he'd still easily defeated both. The two hunters should've planned better for their first solo hunt. "Silver can be deadly to vampires."

"Seriously? I thought you used silver for werewolves…or shapeshifters."

"That's just a myth. For shapeshifters, any of them, you use copper. We have an antidote for silver poisoning. In my experience, some shapeshifters do as well for copper poisoning. It just depends on their pack mentality." Among other things. The book contained a lot of that information. "If you're serious about training, then you need to include time for reading, too."

"I meant what I said. I won't sit on the sidelines like a good, little wife." Odessa snapped her mouth shut. "I mean…" her words trailed off.

A grin spread across his face. Despite what they talked about, he enjoyed that slip-up. They hadn't defined their relationship since discussing the truth. Now seemed like the perfect time to do it.

"You can wipe that stupid grin off your face."

"I don't think I can." Nope, definitely couldn't. Even if he tried, he wouldn't do it. "Whether you meant to say it, the word is out there and I'll never forget it." Hamilton caressed her cheek. In the background, the waves crashed as they swept ashore, playing the perfect symphony. "The truth is…I love you, Dess. Our time apart hasn't changed that. Nothing ever will. And if you'll still have me, I'd very much like to marry you."

"You're either still the smoothest talker I've ever met or…," she closed the small distance between them, wrapped her arms around his waist, and stood on her tiptoes, "I'm completely in love you with and can't imagine my life without you, Hamilton Morck."

"I'm going to take that as a yes," he whispered and claimed her lips in a deep kiss as the cool breeze whipped all around them. The night hadn't gone like he hoped, but it certainly ended on a high note. Now, they just had to survive.

Odessa hooked the white-gold chain around her neck. Seemed like a bad idea to use the old silver one. She checked the position of her engagement ring. While she couldn't wear the halo diamond with curving bands and marquise diamond buds on her finger, it didn't mean she couldn't wear it. Hamilton had selected it for her a few years back. After their conversation last night, she imagined he'd like seeing it on her.

A knock at her door drew her attention from the bedroom mirror. Weren't they meeting downstairs? Had he changed the plan? She picked up her cell phone. No text messages or missed calls. "Alright," she mumbled. Tucking her cell phone in the back pocket of her jeans, she headed toward the door.

Whoever stood on the other side rapped on the door again. "Come on, Odessa. I know you're home."

What the heck? She darted to the front door and yanked it open. Odessa blinked. Sure enough, her brother stared her in the face. As if things couldn't get more complicated. "Leander? What are you doing here?"

"Dad was worried about you." Leander strode past her into the living room. "He said you've been acting weird since you left home."

"That still doesn't explain why you're here in my apartment." Or in New York City, but she didn't tack that on. Her father and brother didn't always respect boundaries. How many times had they done this exact thing when she'd moved in with Hamilton? Too many to count. At least it wasn't at the butt crack of dawn this time.

"I'm in town on business. So, I told Dad I'd check on you while I was here." He turned around, faced her, and crossed his arms. "You look different. Nice. Are you going somewhere?"

"I was going to meet a friend for dinner before work." Odessa shut the front door. None of her neighbors needed to overhear any part of this conversation.

"Alright. Then I'll join you. I wouldn't mind meeting a friend of yours."

God, she loved when her family invited themselves on her outings. "Absolutely not. I'm finding my footing here. I don't need you to act like your overbearing self and ruin things." Not to mention, she couldn't let him see Hamilton. She pulled her cell phone from her back pocket. "I'll just text them and let them know I'll be a few minutes late so we can talk and make plans for another night. How long are you in town for?"

"Claude and I have a meeting tomorrow. So, a few days." Leander narrowed his dark eyes at her. "Now, why don't you want me to meet your friend? Are you hiding something? Dating someone?"

Shit. A meeting with Claude? That explained why her redirection attempt didn't work. Too late to take it back now. Odessa shot a quick text to Hamilton. *Don't come to my building.* Simple and straight to the point. She returned her phone to her back pocket. Since redirection failed, it left her one other option. Mimicking her brother's posture, Odessa folded her arms across her chest and smirked. "Yeah, sure, because that's the only reason it could be, right? Not anything else? Like, I don't know, you storming into my place unannounced as if you own it. Or acting as if I'm incapable of taking care of myself. Couldn't be either of those, right?"

Her brother held up his hands in defeat. "Alright. Point taken." He let out a heavy sigh. "I just wanted to make sure you're okay. The last year has been rough on you. When Dad told me you hung up on him your first night here…" his words trailed off. He pointed to her forehead. "What's that?"

"Nothing." Shit, shit, shit. She'd adjusted her bangs earlier, but it seemed not enough to fully cover the stitches.

"Bullshit!" Leander brushed her hair aside. "What the hell, Odessa? Why are you hiding this? Did someone hurt you?"

"No!" she snapped. Odessa swatted his hand and covered the cut with her hair. Damn it. He had to get all grab-hand on her. "It's nothing. I promise you, I'm fine, Leander."

"Then tell me what happened. I'm not going anywhere until you do." To prove his point, her brother headed toward her living room.

Shit. God, he drove her insane sometimes. "Fine," Odessa grunted. "I tripped and fell down." Her cheeks flushed, and she crossed her arms as if attempting to hide the embarrassment. Yes, it was a blatant lie. Something she'd gotten too damn good at. "Feel better?"

He halted in his steps. "If that's the truth, then yes." His gaze settled on her as an exasperated sigh left his mouth. "I'm sorry, Odessa, but you're my baby sister. You living out here alone has me a little on edge."

"That's sweet, but I promise you, I'm fine, Leander. As to your earlier point, I hung up on Dad because a kitten snuck into my apartment through an open window and startled me." At least that was the truth. As if right on cue, Bard trotted down the hallway from her bedroom and meowed at her brother. The kitten had gotten too comfortable in her bed while she'd dressed. Enough that he hadn't followed her to the door.

"I see. Nothing else?" Her brother asked as he crouched down on his haunches and held his hand out to Bard.

"No." Nothing that she intended to share. She watched as the black kitten turned around and darted back to her bedroom. *God, please don't let that be Hamilton sneaking in again.* Just in case. It was time she got her brother out of here. "Since I have plans tonight, why don't we get together tomorrow night? We can have dinner before I go to work. I can even give you a tour of my new job. Make you feel better about me being here."

Leander rose to his full height of six-foot-four. "I'd like that. I'll come over around seven. Sound good?"

"That's perfect." Yeah, it would take time away from her and Hamilton's plans, but at least her brother wouldn't discover the truth. Without outright asking him to leave, Odessa opened the front door.

"I get the picture, sis. You've got plans. I'll let you get to them." He gave her a warm hug and pressed a tender kiss to her forehead. "I expect to hear all about this friend tomorrow night."

"Promise. I'll share all the gory details." Not a chance. If necessary, she'd tell him about Austin. Hmm, no. Bad idea. Then he'd want to meet the guy. That could lead to all kinds of problems.

"I'll see you tomorrow night." With that, Leander left, pulling the door shut behind him.

Odessa locked the front door, leaned against it, and blew out a breath. She'd gotten her brother to leave, mostly without incident. And without saying or doing anything out of the ordinary. Her defense regarding his reaction to the cut on her head had occurred within reason. A dance they'd done before. Hanging her head, she gripped the back of her neck. God, tomorrow night would prove interesting.

"You managed that well," Hamilton said.

Holding back a groan, Odessa pushed off the door. She closed the distance between them and collected Bard from his arms. "You couldn't have just waited a few minutes?"

"Did you expect me not to respond to a text message like that? You could've been in trouble for all I knew."

"Fair point." She hadn't given him any information. Just hoped he'd listen…for once. Odessa ran her fingers through the kitten's fur. The simple motion relaxed every frayed nerve in her body. "Next time, I'll be more precise." Because something was bound to happen again.

"Alright." Hamilton shoved his hands into the front pockets of his slacks. "You know…this dinner with your brother could be a chance for us."

"For what? Get information on Claude? Uh-uh, no way. If I question anything about their business, Leander will know something's up. And it'll take that much longer to get him out of the city, away from harm. We stick to the plan we already have in motion." It was one thing for her to subject herself to danger. She refused to involve her family. They didn't deserve that.

"What if your brother spots us while we're out to dinner?"

Shit. She hadn't thought about that. Or bothered to find out where he was staying. Hmm. Maybe if she suggested they meet at his hotel tomorrow night, she could find out. Her eyes lit up. "I'll just text him for his hotel information. We can go somewhere that isn't close to it."

"Sure, but what if Claude is using him to get to you? They are meeting tomorrow." Hamilton shrugged. "Hey, you told me to think bigger. I'm considering every possibility."

Odessa cursed under her breath. Yeah, she did. It hadn't crossed her mind the suggestion might bite her in the butt. But it was important to keep her brother safe. "Then we order in for the night and follow the rest of the evening as planned."

"I'm good with that. For the record, I will trail you tomorrow night. Just to be on the safe side." He stepped closer to her, brushed his fingers across her cheek, and pressed a loving kiss to her lips. "Might even give us some true *alone* time tonight before heading to the library."

A shiver swept down her spine. She bit her bottom lip. That sounded like something she could easily get on board with. They could even have dessert first. "I guess we'll just have to see where the night takes us," she replied in a husky tone.

A low growl rumbled in his chest. Hamilton stroked his thumb across the ring dangling from the chain around her neck. "Maybe before it's over, you'll have that back in its rightful place."

The skin-to-skin contact set a blaze off in her lower belly. As much as she yearned to take Hamilton right there in her living room, they required sustenance first. "Maybe." Hamilton could certainly attempt to persuade her. Though it seemed like a better idea to wait until after her brother left New York. It might even be best if she took it off for dinner tomorrow night. Leander hadn't noticed it tonight, but if he spotted it, he'd question it. Even more so if he saw it on her finger. At least at work and around Theodore, she didn't have to worry so much. "Let's get some food ordered. I'm hungry."

Thirteen

"WHO ELSE ARE WE EXPECTING?" Odessa asked her brother as he slid into one side of the red-vinyl booth and she slipped into the other. He'd mentioned a third person to their party, but hadn't said anything about it the entire trip to Bernie's. A restaurant she'd selected with Hamilton's help. It allowed him to watch over her and kept her away from parks controlled by shapeshifters or witches.

"Oh, Claude is joining us. This is certainly an interesting choice for dinner." Her brother set the crayons spread out across the butcher paper aside.

He didn't just say that. Nope. She had to have misheard him. "I'm sorry. Who's coming again?"

"I am," a male voice replied from behind her.

Shit. Odessa swallowed to wet her parched throat and kept the disgust from her face. No doubt Hamilton had seen Claude enter the restaurant they'd chosen. Someplace that was supposed to be safe. Not that she expected him to try anything with so many people around. Bernie's was hopping tonight. She turned around and offered the male a welcoming smile. "Claude. Long time no see."

"Not too long," he responded.

Odessa glanced at her brother, who stood. Leander reached out and shook Claude's hand. "It's good to see you," her brother stated. He gestured to the circular booth. "Do you want the inside?"

Oh, God. Please don't pick that. She didn't want Claude sitting next to her. At least if her brother sat beside her, she could drag him out. This way, she'd be stuck.

"I'd love that." Claude grinned and claimed the inside of the booth next to Odessa.

Son of a bitch. If only her brother knew the truth, he wouldn't do this to her. Not that she could tell him. Because he'd likely do the unthinkable. And even though she could prove it, she'd never risk Hamilton's life like that. One dinner. She could survive one dinner. Hopefully, Hamilton didn't try anything after it was over. Her cell phone buzzed in her pocket.

Leander frowned as he slid in after Claude. "I thought you silenced that."

"I did. Well, I put it on vibrate. Never know when something important might come up." Odessa pulled her phone from her skirt's pocket and checked it. "Just Lucy." Yep, it was Hamilton.

Get out, now! I see him heading inside.

"I'm just going to respond really quickly. Let her know I'll call her later." Setting the sarcasm aside, she typed out a response and sent it off.

Can't. He's sitting right beside me. It'll be fine. Don't do anything stupid. Please.

What else could she say? She'd run and leave her brother behind? Hadn't they already discussed both? Odessa returned her cell phone to her pocket. As much as she'd hated Hamilton's idea last night, only one way to make the best of the situation. "So, Claude. What brings you to New York? I never thought of you as someone who'd leave Solvang. It always seemed…more your pace."

"I had some unfinished business to attend to." Claude dipped his chin in her brother's direction. "When Leander told me earlier the two of you were having dinner, it sounded like an opportunity I didn't want to miss."

"Oh? Have you been in town long, then?" Her brother hadn't protested or given her any kind of strange look. Hopefully, that meant he saw these as nothing more than innocent questions. Not that she expected any kind of detailed response. But she could pick up on nuances in Claude's vague answers.

"Longer than I initially planned, but I suspect I should be able to wrap things up soon."

Before she could ask for more information, their server arrived. Great. Talk about timing. Her cell phone buzzed as the female introduced herself and prattled something off. Odessa dug her phone out of her pocket and checked the new text from Hamilton. Two words: *I won't.* Good. They didn't need to make things worse.

"Odessa," her brother called out.

"What?"

"Drink?"

"Oh, right. Sorry." She'd gotten distracted. Odessa flicked her gaze to the female. "Can I get a glass of your House Red and a water, please?"

"Of course. Are you folks ready to order? Or do you need a few minutes?" the female asked.

"A few minutes sounds good. Though I would like an order of mozzarella sticks," Odessa replied. She'd looked over the menu earlier. Part of her plan to make dinner go quickly and smoothly. Not that she'd prepared for an uninvited guest.

The server nodded and left their table.

"I hope you don't intend to be on that thing all night long," her brother commented.

"Not at all. Lucy just sent me a brief reply." She tucked her phone in her pocket. She didn't expect it to go off again. At least not until later. Well after, she and her brother parted ways.

"I didn't know you still spoke to her." Leander steepled his fingers together. "Wasn't the point of you moving out here to leave your past behind?"

Odessa snickered. "You know she lives here in New York, right? Not to mention, she is my best friend. We're going to talk." Why did her brother have such a problem with the female? Something he'd never expressed before.

"I wasn't aware she was here. What exactly do you discuss?"

"Ah, well, I told her about this guy from my building, if you must know." And she'd now brought Austin into the conversation. Not that she'd mentioned her date with him. Something she'd absolutely keep to herself. "I thought he seemed like her type," Odessa tacked on before her brother could ask. It was best to get ahead of him and redirect their discussion. She glanced at Claude. "The business that brought you into town. Does it have something to do with why you two met earlier?"

"Not at all," Claude said. "They're actually two separate endeavors. Though I'm certain both will go off without a hitch."

"You sound rather confident. What if they don't?" She half-shrugged and eyed her brother. "I don't wish failure of any kind on you, but things happen."

"We have a contingency plan in place should something fall through," her brother replied.

That didn't sound like a good thing. Though she was certain Leander hadn't meant it that way. As for Claude…he likely did. She hoped he hadn't pulled her brother into something supernatural. Not that she'd put it past him. If what they believed was true, he'd used humans once to do his dirty work. What would stop him from doing it again? "You'll have to tell me more about this business deal. I'd love to help you see it through, Leander."

"It's just the purchase of a couple of buildings. Nothing you can really do on that front. But if anything arises, I'll keep your offer in mind."

Of course, he would. As much as she wanted to know more about these negotiations, if she pushed too much, her brother would question her motives. Anything that involved Claude couldn't be on the up and up. What kind of building could he wish to purchase? That concerned her, but no way would she get anywhere further regarding their dealings.

"I see you're wearing your engagement ring," Claude pointed out.

Her brother narrowed his eyes at her. "Didn't you take that off before you moved? I thought you were going to stop wearing that. Move forward from the past, right? That's what you said, so you should stick to that."

Damn it. It had completely slipped her mind that she still had it on. Odessa opened her mouth to offer an explanation and snapped it shut. No. She refused to play Claude's game any longer. Or defend herself further to her brother. Obviously, Claude had joined their dinner to stir some trouble. Enough was enough. She ground her jaw and expelled a slow breath. "You've been nothing but judgmental since you showed up at my apartment last night. Just because you're five years older than me doesn't mean you can come in here and start giving me orders. I'm not a child, Leander. I'm an adult, fully capable of making my own decisions and living my own life. So, I suggest you stop trying to run it for me, fixing problems that don't exist, and focus on your own issues. Otherwise, I'll happily get a cab and leave you here. Understood?"

"I'm just worried about you, Odessa. Nothing more," her brother replied.

"No." She slammed her hand down on the checkered tablecloth and pointed a finger at him. "Don't you dare use that as an excuse. There is nothing for you to worry about." Out of her periphery, she caught sight of their server returning with their drinks. None too soon. She needed the wine more than ever. "Now, I suggest we order our dinner and try to enjoy the rest of the evening."

"Alright. I concede."

"Good." Just to settle whatever rift Claude might continue to put between her and her brother, she shot daggers at the male, warning him to knock it off. Hopefully, he got the picture and the rest of their meal went smoothly. Even if she had to make small talk with the two of them. *That* she could easily handle. Not that silence would bother her. Either way, she was taking control of the situation.

Hamilton surveyed the restaurant entrance from across the street. He'd positioned himself in a tree, though he maintained his invisibility. It simply gave him the best vantage point. It even allowed him to hear the entire conversation that took place between Odessa, Leander, and Claude, which had settled into something mimicking pleasantries after his fiancée's earlier outburst. Not that he could've been prouder of her.

At the moment, he watched as Odessa and Leander got into a cab to head to the library. As for his uncle…a broad smile crossed his face as Claude strode toward the park. Wasn't that convenient? He climbed down, taking his time to make it to the bottom. The last thing he wanted was to draw attention to his movements. Yeah, he'd told Odessa he wouldn't do anything stupid. That didn't mean he wouldn't take advantage of Claude's presence.

Hamilton perched on a branch about thirty feet from the ground. He sat silently as Claude passed by the tree and shoved his hands into the pockets of his coat. Although it looked as if his uncle didn't have any weapons on him, Hamilton knew better. The man went nowhere without at least one. Something small and easily concealed. While hunters had extensive hearing, it didn't compare to that of a vampire. Still, better not to risk jumping down too soon. Even though leaves blanketed the pathway, they wouldn't do much to dampen the sound of his landing.

Instead, he continued his descent and moved to the next limb, getting as low as possible. Hamilton leaped to the sidewalk and landed with a soft crack. He lifted his eyes, pushed up to his full height of six-foot-seven-inches, and located his uncle. The male paused in his steps. Shit.

"Ah, so you were watching," Claude muttered over his shoulder and slowly turned around. "Why don't you come out to play, nephew? We have so much to catch up on."

It didn't matter he'd thrown away the element of surprise. This was a chance he couldn't pass up. Without dropping his invisibility, Hamilton took deliberate steps forward and closed rank on his uncle. As he crept along, he extended his claws and fangs.

"You don't intend to make this a fair fight? That's alright. It doesn't have to be fair. I killed you once. I can certainly do it again." His uncle unbuttoned his coat.

The guy actually challenged him. Not that he'd take the bait, especially when he could strategically attack the guy. Hamilton stood a few feet from Claude. He sprung into the air, dropped his invisibility, and struck his uncle across the face. Blood splattered all over his suit. Before the male could react, he followed it with an uppercut to the jaw and sent Claude flying.

Claude hit the ground, touching down with his feet. He skidded to a stop. With a smirk, he charged at Hamilton, who ran toward him in return.

Hamilton sidestepped to the left, but it didn't prevent Claude from stabbing him in the shoulder. As he slid by him, he sliced the side of his uncle's stomach open. Although it didn't do much damage, it didn't stop crimson from spewing everywhere. The male elbowed him in the back of the head. He stumbled forward a few steps, but quickly caught his footing.

He turned around and Claude drove the heel of his boot into his leg, knocking him to his knees. This wasn't over. It couldn't end like this. Not when he had so much to live for.

"I think I'll enjoy this even more than I did the first time." Claude drew a dagger from his coat and hauled it up overhead. The male howled in pain. Reaching over his shoulder, he yanked a dagger from his shoulder blade and tossed it aside. It skittered across the sidewalk.

What the hell? Where had that…? Hamilton spotted his sire race toward them. Taking advantage of the distraction, he rammed his claws into his uncle's chest. Claude slammed his fist into Hamilton's ball socket with a loud sickening pop. He fell backward onto the ground, ripping his claws from his uncle's body.

Without hesitation, Claude took off.

"Son of a bitch," Hamilton grunted. The perfect opportunity and it had slipped through his fingers just like that. All of this could've been over and done.

"He's gone." Theo held out his hand.

Not that he accepted it. He didn't need help to get to his feet. Even if he moved a little slower. "Why'd you do that? I had him." Hamilton eyed the place on his shoulder where his uncle stabbed him. Silver radiated up his arm, bulging his veins. "Shit."

"Saved you? You're welcome. Don't worry. I won't do it again." With a derisive snort, his sire produced an antidote-filled syringe. "Here. Looks like you could use this."

Now that he would take. He removed the safety cover with his teeth, spit it out, and drove the needle into his arm. "Thank you." Hamilton collected the orange cap from the ground and handed both back to Theo. Normally, he'd handle their disposal, but he had to pop his shoulder back into place. It wouldn't hurt nearly as much as silver poisoning. "How'd you know where to find me?"

"Your female. She sent me a text and asked me to check on you. Seems she knows you well." Theo recapped the needle and tucked it away. "Come. We should begin our travel to the library. I've got a suit for you in the car so you can change."

Of course, she did. He'd made her a promise, and she expected him not to keep it. Hamilton shook his head. With a slight grunt, he yanked on his arm and got everything situated. "Did she tell you to do that? Bring me a suit?"

"No. That I thought of all on my own." His sire clasped his hands together at the small of his back and started walking.

Right. So much for their faith in him. Something they could discuss later. Right now, he had a date to keep.

"Why would you do something like that?" Odessa demanded as she and Hamilton entered her apartment. She shut the door behind him. "You have help readily available and you go after him alone."

"I don't need help. I can defeat him on my own," he retorted. "But you don't agree, do you?"

And now it all made sense. She'd trained with him yesterday morning. Even after all their work at the library, nothing altered her belief in his abilities. Odessa put her purse and coat up and then closed the distance between them. She took his hands in her own. "I absolutely believe you can defeat him, but only if you set your ego aside. It's your worst enemy. Always has been. The way to win this is with strategy and not taking his bait. And you know that. You're stronger, faster, and smarter than him. I guarantee *he* knows that. Otherwise, he wouldn't have to play a game. So, stop playing up his strengths and focus on yours."

Hamilton gripped the back of his neck with a heavy sigh. "I'm just so afraid of losing you. Sometimes, I can't see straight."

"That doesn't make it okay." There had to be another way for her to state this. Something that showed him how important it was for him to lose his ego. "I love you, Hamilton. I want to marry you. But I can't do any of that if we don't both come out of this alive."

"I want that, too." He beamed as he leaned down and brushed a soft kiss across her lips.

"Then we'll make it happen. Together." Odessa slid her hands up his arms, curled her fingers around the back of his neck, and fused their lips together. Despite the long night they already had, she couldn't think of a more perfect way for them to end it. Or celebrate what they'd accomplished. "Mmm…maybe we should take this to the shower. Conserve some water and all that jazz."

"It's like you read my mind." He grabbed her around the waist, tossed her over his shoulder, and started down the hallway.

She squealed. "Hamilton! Put me down!" Her gaze fell to his nice, round ass. This was a good view. Balling up his jacket in her fist for additional support, she smacked his ass cheek.

"I thought you wanted down," he said with a slight chuckle. "Two can play that game." With a loud whack, his palm connected with her ass.

A shudder swept through her body. Holy shit. Her body hadn't ever responded like it just did before. She bit her bottom lip. God, she wanted more. With her free hand, Odessa squeezed his butt cheek and then swatted it again.

"Hmm, you like that, huh, Dess?" Hamilton brought his hand down on her behind, and then rubbed a slow circle along her other cheek before connecting his palm with it again.

Odessa moaned. Fire speared her body, shooting straight to her core. Being intimate with him as a vampire was like discovering a whole new world. Each time they came together was unlike anything they'd experienced before. Would it always be like this? She didn't know, but she couldn't wait to find out.

Opening the door to the bathroom, he rounded the corner, set her down on her feet, claimed her lips with his own, and kicked the bathroom door shut. Without breaking off the kiss once, they quickly worked to strip each other of their clothes. Their shoes got tossed, landing somewhere on the floor. Hurriedly, they got his suit and her skirt and blouse off.

Hamilton gripped her ass, lifted her, carried her over to the shower stall, and lazily stroked his fingers up and down her spine. Goosebumps crawled across her skin as shivers shot straight to her core.

She wrapped her legs tighter around his waist as she curled her fingers around his neck. Mesmerized over this perfect specimen of pure, silky-smooth, unadulterated muscle, she ran her fingers up his forearms and over the curve of his biceps. Odessa groaned. God, he felt like pure heaven. Her palms continued their trek across the multiple dips and nuances of his shoulders and back. The large bulge pressed against the juncture between her legs, making her ache with need.

The shower came on. Not that she cared too much about it. They weren't inside the stall yet. Right now, all that mattered was ditching the last of the clothing that kept them from being skin-to-skin.

Hamilton unhooked her bra, carefully removed it from her body, and flung it across the bathroom. He brushed his thumb across one of her nipples and she moaned into the kiss. His fingers skimmed down her sides as his lips left hers and skated down her throat. He latched onto one of her nipples and sucked hard.

"Oh, God!" She arched her neck as she dug her nails into the back of his arms. Holy fuck, the things he was doing to her made the inferno burn hotter. She dragged her fingers down the taut, defined shape of his back. He flicked his tongue across her other nipple, sending her body on a rollercoaster ride. Her heart raced as she gyrated against his hot, rigid length.

Steam slowly filled the bathroom. The tips of Hamilton's fingers danced across her silk panties, inching lower. "Drop your legs."

Odessa bit her bottom lip and did as he instructed. Their gazes met as her feet touched the floor. She hooked her thumbs into the sides of her panties and slowly slipped them down her legs. His dark-green eyes were so glossy, but the look in them…she could see the hunger he had for her. Tugging the shower curtain aside, she climbed into the stall and crooked a finger at him.

He yanked his boxers off. There he stood in front of her, gloriously naked. Head to toe, powerfully built and robust. Hamilton stepped over their pile of clothes, following her into the shower. He yanked the curtain back into place and shut them in together.

Her tongue darted out across her bottom lip. "Absolutely gorgeous."

Taking a few steps forward, the corner of his mouth curled into a half-smile. "I was going to say the same thing." He crouched down, hooked an arm underneath her knee, and fused his mouth to her sex. Water slapped at his broad shoulders, spraying all around them.

"Oh, God," Odessa moaned. She shot her hand out, gripped the shower wall, and rocked her sex against his tongue as he drove at her hard and fast. He rubbed her clit with this thumb. She'd already been close to an orgasm before he devoured her. It wouldn't take long for her to come now.

Their eyes locked. Hamilton relentlessly rubbed her clit, while increasing the rhythm of his tongue, driving it into her repeatedly. His hold on her thighs tightened. She dug her heel into his shoulder as her toes curled. Her core tensed as a massive orgasm slammed through her body, exploding over his tongue.

With an intense growl, he bore down and drove at her ferociously without stopping once until she finished. Slowly, Hamilton unfurled his grip from her thigh and stood up as he stroked the outside of his lips with his fingers, then licked them clean. "Best dessert I've ever had."

Holy fucking shit. That statement combined with the vivid color of his eyes; she'd swear he wanted to do it again. That was seriously hot. Before any response left her mouth, he pressed his lips to hers, pulling her into a slow, deep kiss.

Wrapping his hands around her waist, he slid his hands down to her ass. In one swift move, he lifted her, spread her thighs, and pushed the head of his cock against her entrance. Then he rocked his pelvis back, and the tip of his shaft slipped just inside her folds. With one more swing of his hips, she fully sheathed his girth.

Odessa slapped one hand against the shower wall and dug her nails into his shoulder with the other. She slid her feet over his ass cheeks, gripping tightly onto him.

Hamilton fisted a handful of her hair. He pistoned in and out of her sex. Each stroke of his rigid length along her vaginal walls sent jolts of lightning straight to her core. The high he'd brought her down from not too long ago built all over again. It was like the high of opening a new book on loop-to-loop.

And fuck if she didn't want more.

She spread her thighs further apart, allowing his cock to go deeper. They both moaned into the kiss. Odessa raked her nails down his back. As the power and rhythm of his thrusts increased, she rocked her hips, meeting him thrust for thrust.

Sex had always been enjoyable, but it hadn't ever been anything like this. The way their bodies moved together, the way his chest pressed against her breasts, the synchronized pounding of their hearts—it built an endless heatwave between them. Water sluiced down both of their bodies, intensifying the sensations between them.

They were so connected, functioning as one.

Hamilton broke off the kiss and rested his forehead against hers. His fingers dug into her flesh as he drilled his cock into her sex harder and faster. "Come with me, Dess. Come with me."

Odessa cried out his name. Her thighs tensed, her toes curled, and a massive orgasm speared through her body. Hamilton grunted, slapping a hand against the tiled wall with a loud crack. His eyes narrowed, and he pounded into her as an orgasm punched out of his cock. The room erupted into a mixture of growls and screams of ecstasy as they rode their releases out together.

She couldn't say how long it lasted or how much time passed before their bodies stilled. Hamilton buried his face in the crook of her neck, panting heavily. She gingerly ran her fingers up and down his spine. Ragged breaths left her mouth as the two of them stood there unmoving.

Hamilton lifted his head and brushed a tender kiss across her lips. "I love you, Odessa."

The corners of her mouth tilted into a soft smile. "I love you, too, Hamilton." She didn't know how things could get any better than they were at that moment. Then again, she'd never thought she'd be happy again. And she was. More so than she imagined possible.

fourteen

"YEAH, THIS LOOKS LIKE A dive where he'd stay," Hamilton commented as he took in the sight of the decaying motel. He'd seen campsites that looked in better condition. Pamphlets for nearby takeout restaurants scattered the parking lot. None of the numbered doors he spotted had gotten an upgrade in years. They still used keys to unlock them.

"At least breaking in should be easy," Odessa said. She squeezed his hand. "Come on. The room can't be any worse. It's all the information we have to go on."

The motel itself comprised two floors, about twenty rooms on each level. He spotted one corner where a couple of vending machines still sat, provided they worked. Gripping the back of his neck, he let out an exasperated sigh. "Alright."

They strolled across the semi-empty parking lot toward the staircase. His uncle had occupied room twenty-five, dead center of the second floor. With the few cars he noted, they wouldn't have to worry about nosy neighbors. Mostly. He expected anyone here wouldn't care about them scoping out one room. Theo had already broken into it.

"You get the sense this places rents by the hour." Odessa shuddered.

"Probably." He smirked as they ascended the staircase. A door at the top of the stairs opened. Two people exited. Both the male and female had mussed up hair and reeked of sex. She had on the shortest dress he'd ever seen. Even Odessa didn't wear anything like that. Hamilton canted his head. Though, if she did, she'd look damn good.

"Dare I even ask?"

"Oh, I'm sure if you try hard enough, you can figure it out." She'd read his mind before. Well, so to speak. He snickered as her eyes widened. "Maybe for one of our date nights." Hamilton half-shrugged. "Might be fun."

Odessa chuckled. "Maybe."

It didn't sound like it would take much to convince her to wear something daring. They stopped in front of the room Theo told them about and he rapped on the door with his knuckles. The door opened. Theo grimaced, yanked a handkerchief from his front jacket pocket, and wiped off his hand. He cocked an eyebrow at the male. "That bad?"

"This place is horrendous. How anyone other than cockroaches can use these rooms is beyond me."

Waving a hand in front of her face, Odessa frowned. "I'll say. This place stinks."

The scent of stale cigarettes comingled with mildew wafted in the air. And he was fairly certain he caught a whiff of piss. "Yeah. Hunters hole up in a place like this. Definitely smells like Claude."

"Then let's see what we can find and get out of here." Odessa glanced between Hamilton and Theo. "Unless either of you brought a gas mask with you, I suggest we open a window."

"I'll take care of that," he said before his sire could pipe up. The guy looked as if he preferred not to touch anything more than he already had. Hamilton stepped into the room, tugged on the thick drapes, and nearly gagged on the plume of dust that erupted forth. It took him a moment to clear the awful taste from his mouth before he opened the window. "That should air it some."

His fiancée entered the room behind him. "There doesn't even appear to be much in here. Are we sure he stayed here?"

"I confirmed the name attached to the room with the day manager earlier today," Theo replied. "He said that they had paid the rent through until the end of next week."

"That seems to track," Hamilton said. "At least if we're to believe what he told you, Dess, is accurate." Despite some things he'd heard in that conversation, nothing Claude uttered sounded like a lie. "Check the dresser, closet, and behind any of the furniture. If Claude stayed here, we'll find some trace he's left behind."

No one had made either of the two beds. Muted stains covered the blankets. Not something anyone with normal eyesight would really notice. Or they simply overlooked. Hamilton crossed the room, ducked between the beds, and searched the nightstand. He removed a stack of papers stuck together. None of them provided any insight. They had nonsensical notes scribbled. "Hey, Dess, does the language on any of these look familiar?"

She eyed the papers he held in his hands. "It doesn't even look like a language. Just scribbles." Leaving his side, she strode around the bed to the closet and opened the door. "There's nothing in here," Odessa called out. "Just a bunch of empty hangers."

"Nothing here either." Hamilton tossed the stack on the bed. He peered over at Theo, who merely shook his head at him. Dragging a hand down his face, he focused on his fiancée.

Odessa turned. She cocked her head and walked over to the armoire. Gripping the side, she pulled it away from the wall a bit. "Um, guys."

Both he and his sire headed to where she stood. Hamilton scanned over the extensive collection of photographs taped to the wall. There were so many. Odessa appeared in most of them, which looked as if Claude had taken them from a distance. They comprised her apartment, the front of her building, the library, and even restaurants she'd visited. A few included him. The time they'd spent together and while he spied on her. "He's been watching us for at least a couple of weeks."

"Yes, but that's not all I can tell from these." Odessa pointed out the ones around the front of her building. "A lot of the photographs are far away, but these aren't. He's close. Not that I ever saw him."

"What does that mean?" Theo asked.

"He's taken up residence somewhere near my building. There are a few places across the street from me that are completely uninhabited. What if he holed up in one of them?"

Hamilton folded his arms across his chest. "It would make sense. But how many buildings are we talking about?" They only had a handful of days to locate Claude and present his head to the council. It had taken them too long to find this place. Time wasn't on their side.

"I don't know for sure. Maybe if we take these photographs with us, we can analyze them further to pinpoint his exact location."

"That sounds like a good idea." Not that he knew much about cameras or a telephoto lens. Except they'd have to identify that first.

Odessa squeezed his arm. "Hey. I know it's not much, but it's better than nothing."

"I know." He scrubbed a hand down his face. No matter how hard they tried, Claude always seemed one step ahead of them. This hadn't turned out any better than his attempt to kill the guy. "I guess I was just hoping we'd find more of a breadcrumb."

"We'll keep looking until we take care of business. We're not giving up." She kissed his cheek. "Alright?"

Hamilton draped an arm across her shoulders and tucked her against his side. "I believe you." They wouldn't quit. Not until he killed and beheaded Claude.

Odessa locked the library's front doors. With the work she'd done with Hamilton and Theodore over the last few hours, their research into the photographs had proven fruitful. They still didn't have all the answers, but they were closer. Theodore left a half-hour earlier, so it gave her and

Hamilton some time alone together. "I know I have to come back in the morning, but I wish we could fast track some of this."

"Theo and I could always just scout the buildings across from you for Claude, but if he caught on, then he'd just disappear again. And we'd have to start over."

"That doesn't sound very positive." She smirked. He couldn't have just given her a simple answer. Tugging on the metallic door handle, she jiggled it and ensured it had completely locked. "What? We have a lot of precious items to protect."

"Does this mean when all of this is over, you expect me to follow through on your suggestions?"

"Oh, absolutely. I also expect a raise and more control regarding what we order." Odessa winked. The latter she added in jest, not that she'd argue if he agreed.

Hamilton took her hand in his and threaded their fingers together as they descended the stairs toward the parking lot. "Does this mean when we get married, you'll take my last name?"

"Which one? Kring? Or Morck? The first carries a lot of baggage. And the second…well, it's kind of ostentatious, don't you think?" They'd had this conversation in the past. Back then, she'd agreed to take his last name. Now, it seemed too weird to become Mrs. Kring. Especially considering their plans. But would Morck be better?

"Definitely Morck. Unless you don't really want the control you mentioned. That is how it works, right? We get married, you take my last name, and what's mine becomes yours."

"Except I don't have to take your name for that to happen. It's the natural order once we're married," Odessa teased. She couldn't recall the last time they joked around like this. With all that happened over the last few days, it was nice not to focus on the serious. It would still be there when they got home.

"So, right now I'm your boss, but after we're hitched, you become my boss? That doesn't sound right."

"You're right. Except I'm already your boss." She threw her head back in laughter as Hamilton pursed his lips at her. The look on his face said it all. They hit the bottom stair and headed for the lone car in the lot. Her heels clicked against the slightly uneven pavement. "You know we really share the power, don't you?"

"And now you're patronizing me." He shook his head and buried it in his palm.

"I'd never do that," Odessa uttered, drawing out her words. She shouldn't enjoy teasing him so much, but she couldn't help it. Not when it made him fake pout like that.

"You're doing it again," Hamilton proclaimed. "I don't know what I'm going to do with you." He let out a soft chuckle and pressed a kiss to her temple. "Actually, I think I do. As you said, we share the power. And all this teasing makes me think a good punishment is in order."

If he planned to spank her again, well, she could absolutely handle that. A slight shudder swept through her. "You might be onto something."

Hamilton wrapped an arm around her waist, tucked her in close to his side, and whispered in her ear, "I know I am."

"It's a good thing Grayson left the Jeep." Because she couldn't wait—two males stepped out from behind the SUV, giving her and Hamilton pause. Each one had on black clothes, covered from head-to-toe. The same military gear she'd seen the hunters wearing a few days ago. Certainly not something they needed right now. At least this time, she was better prepared. Not that she'd move just yet.

"Really, guys? I'm getting a complex here." He released his hold on Odessa, stepping in front of her a bit.

Yeah, she'd only trained with him and Theodore for a couple of days, but that didn't mean she required his protection. Though, she could take advantage of her fiancé's actions. Odessa hugged herself, slipping a hand into the hidden compartment of her purse.

One man tore the covering from his head. His dark eyes narrowed at Hamilton. "I used to think when a hunter died, he stayed dead. Lo' and behold I find out you're still upright and breathing."

"I suppose I shouldn't be surprised you're here, Einarr," Hamilton replied. "You never could let the past go."

That name? It sounded familiar. Her eyes flicked back and forth between the hunters. The book. It had mentioned the male's family and their history with the Krings. A rivalry. Yeah, no surprise at all.

"That's ironic, coming from you." Einarr smirked. "What? Didn't think I'd recognize the female standing by your side? I'm sure you hoped we wouldn't. But don't worry," he gestured to Odessa, "while I'm dealing with you, my associate, here, will handle her."

Hamilton growled and pushed Odessa behind him more. "Leave her out of this."

"Not a chance," the hunter stated as he removed two curved blades from his back.

This man and his incessant need to protect her was absolutely going to piss her off. So what, if she only had a couple days of training? It was better than nothing. Besides, she'd come prepared. Odessa pulled the hand gun out of her purse's secret compartment and dropped her purse to the ground. She kicked it with the back of her heel, flipped the safety off the gun, took a few steps to the left, and aimed.

The two hunters charged forward, one at her and one at Hamilton. Damn, they moved faster than she expected. Odessa shot at the male racing toward her and missed. Shit. She fired off another round and stumbled backward a couple of steps. It had more kickback than she remembered. Shit. Her opponent disappeared. Where'd he—? The guy grabbed the gun from her hands, tossed it down, and socked her in the gut.

Fuck, that hurt. Not that she could think about the pain. As Odessa gasped, drawing air deep into her lungs, she balled up her fists and placed them in front of her face.

"At least you'll die with dignity." The male cracked his neck, first one side, and then the other. He brought his fists up. "Let's see what you got."

"Do all of you normally talk this much?" It was a rhetorical question.

One that gave her time to adjust her stance for maximum impact. This wasn't a fight she could afford to lose. Without waiting for a response, Odessa threw a jab. Although she'd hit him square in the jaw, it didn't do much. Just meant she had to try harder.

The hunter swung at her. She sidestepped and punched him in the nose. He staggered a bit as blood trickled down his cheeks. The male shrugged it off and surged forward.

Only one way she'd win this. If she took advantage of his movement. And got a little dirty. Odessa struck him in the side and kicked him in the groin.

Grabbing his balls, the male grunted, "You bitch." He lunged at her, punched her twice, forcing her backward. Before she could react, he backhanded her across the face, busting her bottom lip open. The guy thrust his hand out and grabbed Odessa around the throat. Lifting her up off the ground, he pulled her in close. "I'm going to enjoy watching the life drain from you."

That didn't have the effect she'd hoped. The hold he had around her throat tightened. Odessa thrashed around, kicking out as best she could. Her feet dangled in the air. It didn't do a damn bit of good as she flailed about. The more she slapped at his arm, the harder it got to breathe. Her lungs constricted and her surroundings got hazy. Shit. She wouldn't last long like this. How did she get out of it?

Grayson's words replayed in her mind, *They are stronger and faster, so that means you have to fight smarter. Don't fight fair.*

That thing he'd stuck in her belt. Smacking at the hunter's arm with her one hand, Odessa slid the other to the inside of her leather belt. She curled her fingers around something long and cylindric. Without hesitation, she jammed it into the side of the hunter's neck.

Blood spewed everywhere as he let go of her, dropping her to the ground. She landed on her back against the pavement with a loud groan. Pain radiated up her spine. Odessa coughed, desperately trying to steady her breathing. Rolling onto her side, she attempted to alleviate the agony coursing through her body. That hurt way more than expected.

The hunter fell, hitting the ground with a thud. He wheezed, drawing in sharp breaths. His fingers scraped against the asphalt.

Slowly, she sat up. As the hunter she'd fought struggled for air and hacked up blood, she angled her body and peered at Hamilton. He swiped his claws across Einarr's chest, shredding the guy's shirt. Crimson freckled the male's flesh. Not that he appeared to notice.

Bang!

A stinging sensation swept through her gut. It was like someone with an iron fist punched her in the stomach through her back. Her gaze fell to her belly. Blood seeped through her white blouse.

"Odessa!" Hamilton screamed.

As she collapsed backward, she caught sight of the fallen hunter's hand. The male had shot her…with her own gun.

"Bastard," she croaked out. Tugging on the hem of her blouse, she pressed her palm against the wound and hissed. Fuck, that burned. But she couldn't ease up any. It was the only way she might survive this. The pressure inside her body intensified. It filled up like someone had inflated a balloon on the left side of her belly. She coughed up blood. It trickled down her cheeks and chin.

Fuck. This was bad. Really bad. This was it—the end of her life. Tears welled in the corners of her eyes. Oh, God. How would her father survive without her? How would Hamilton? They'd only just found one another again. After everything they'd faced together over the last ten years, all the loss…she didn't want to leave him. *God, please…please, I need more time,* Odessa prayed.

There was so much she hadn't done. Not that she cared about living for herself. Her eyes flicked to Hamilton as he skidded to his knees beside her. There were so many things she hadn't told him. Since the day they'd met, he made her want to live. He taught her to enjoy the little things life offered. On days the world deflated what confidence she had, he lifted her up. Hamilton encouraged her in so many ways. She couldn't leave him without telling him all he'd done for her. But what could she say to let him know the truth? Odessa lifted a shaky hand. "Love…you…"

"I love you, too, but you're not dying on me today," Hamilton said as he gripped her hand. He adjusted his position, carefully elevated her head, and eased it onto his knee. "I can heal you. All you have to do is drink." Baring his fangs, he sank them into his wrist. "Just drink."

His blood would heal her? She recalled reading that among the vampire myths she'd researched. Their gazes met. Although his wrist hovered over her mouth, permission lingered in his dark-green eyes. It was a calculated risk. Did she take a chance with forever? Or let it all end, here and now?

Odessa wrapped her lips around Hamilton's wrist. She stroked her tongue across his flesh, swallowing the copper nectar before she even recognized what choice she'd made.

fifteen

HAMILTON ROLLED OVER, HIS HAND plopping on the empty side of the bed. Something soft and furry swatted at his fingers. He cracked an eye open. Where was Odessa? All he spotted was a black kitten using his digits as play toys. "Stop it, Bard," he mumbled. Scrubbing a hand down his face, he yawned and cracked his jaw as he fully came around.

Last night had been long for both him and Odessa. He definitely wouldn't forget it soon.

"Where the hell did you get a gun?" Hamilton asked as he pulled Odessa to her feet. Thank God she'd accepted his blood. Otherwise, she may not have survived that gunshot wound. Not without help quicker rather than later. He had limited knowledge of those kinds of injuries. Hunters rarely used such grotesque weapons.

"Grayson gave it to me," Odessa replied. "Same with that stabby thing. He said they'd serve me well."

Of course, she'd gotten it from the butler. It certainly shouldn't surprise him. The male had served the Morck family for decades. Perhaps longer. He wasn't entirely positive on the timeframe. Just that he'd joined the family years ago. "Did he show you how to use it? Or just give you a few pointers? Because you nearly died."

"Yes, he showed me what to do. I did pretty damn good for someone who's only gone to the shooting range twice. Now, calm down. I'm fine."

Hamilton gripped the back of his neck and propped a hand on his hip. Sure, he'd calm down as soon as she admitted the gun was dangerous. Not something he saw happening. Peering at the car, which had at least two bullet holes, he blew out an exasperated breath and smirked. "You need more practice. Come on. Let's go."

"We can't just leave their bodies here," Odessa retorted.

"I'll call Grayson. He can handle clean up." His collection needed more heads. All something he planned to present to the council. It would definitely get them off his hide for a while. In theory, anyway. Hamilton held his hand out to his fiancée.

"Really? He does that?" She glanced from one dead hunter to the other.

"Yes, he does. Right now, you and I need to go." Hanging out here and waiting for Grayson wasn't a good idea. The male didn't need them to linger.

Chewing on her bottom lip, she hesitantly took his hand. "Wait. My purse." She walked away, collected it, and reclaimed his hand. "Where are we going?"

He gently tugged her toward the car. "To your place so you can pack a bag and to grab Bard. You're staying with me from now on. Before you argue with me, this is the second time we've been attacked. I won't chance a third."

Thankfully, she hadn't disagreed with his assessment of the situation. Hamilton sat upright, stretched, and eyed the velvet drapes pulled tight across the window. The shutters hadn't opened yet. It still had to be daylight. He scratched the top of Bard's head and glanced at the clock. Almost five o'clock. He had about an hour before sunset.

Odessa had gone to work for a few hours earlier this morning, though he expected her back by now. No matter how much he insisted she stay home, she refused. He figured she would've laid back down with him when she'd returned, but that hadn't happened. His pulse quickened. Maybe she opted to head straight to the dining room. It was time for their first meal of the evening. That made sense. Perfect sense.

Hamilton tossed the covers aside and climbed out of bed. He disappeared inside the bathroom connected to his bedroom. One of the many things he liked about the house—privacy. He quickly took care of business. As he washed his hands, he stared at his reflection in the mirror and drew his eyebrows together.

The lack of Odessa's presence in bed didn't mean anything was wrong. She simply hadn't gotten home yet. How many times had she lost track of time in the past? Several. It was nothing for her to get so involved in her work that she didn't notice how much time had passed. This knot in his stomach held no meaning. Just an overreaction on his part.

He finished up in the bathroom, walked into the bedroom, and headed straight for the closet. Normally, he took his time getting dressed for the evening. Tonight, he didn't want to waste a second. He'd find Odessa downstairs, waiting for him at the table.

Last night's fiasco gave them some leads on Claude to follow up. Einarr wasn't as smart as the male always believed. Grayson discovered the guy's cell phone while cleaning up the parking lot mess. It had proven useful and offered more than they'd found on their own. He might actually deliver his uncle's head to the council sooner rather than later.

Hamilton selected a burgundy dress shirt, a black velluto waistcoat, jacket, and matching slacks. To complete the ensemble, he picked a pocket square from the top drawer of his dresser. Usually, he didn't care much about how he paired a Sebastian Cruz suit. He preferred practical over expensive, but tonight he wanted to look his best for Odessa.

This would do the job.

It didn't take him long to get fully dressed—shoes and all. Shoving his cell phone in his pocket, he strode out of his bedroom and made his way downstairs with Bard trailing him. His muscles tightened. Strange. Nothing more than the usual noises reached his ears—clinking glassware and the ruffled sound of newspaper pages being shifted. Had Odessa not come home yet?

Stopping in the dining room entry way, he glanced around the nearly empty table. Only Theo occupied it. Their butler stepped out of the kitchen with a tray in his hand. Every part of his body tensed. Where the hell was Odessa? Hamilton shoved his hands in the pockets of his pants. "Grayson, shouldn't you have gone to pick up Odessa?"

"Miss Black advised she would message me when she wished to be collected from the shooting range."

"The shooting range?" Hamilton pinched the bridge of his nose. She'd gone somewhere they hadn't discussed. Great. The knowledge that she'd do something like this must've registered in the back of his mind. It certainly explained the hollow sensations in the pit of his stomach. "When did you drop her off?"

"A couple of hours ago, Master Morck."

Hamilton's cell phone dinged. He dug it out of his pocket. "That's probably her now."

"There you go. Nothing to fret over," Theo commented as he flipped to another page of the paper.

"How'd you even…" his words trailed off. He read the text message a second time. A low growl rumbled in his chest. Hamilton ran toward the front door.

A chair fell over, smacking against the floor. Theo darted in front of him and slammed his hand against the heavy oak door. "Where are you going?"

"Get out of the way!" He pushed his sire, but only knocked the male's arm from the door. Not that he would stop attempting to move him until he could walk out of the house. Claude had to die. Now.

"That's enough!" Theo shoved Hamilton, who stumbled backward a few steps. "If you go outside now, you'll burn! Now, what is going on? Why are you doing this?"

"He has her!" Hamilton dragged his hand through his hair, gripping it tightly in his palm. "Claude took her!" He held his cell phone out to his sire, revealing the text and picture of Odessa tied up, dangling from the ceiling with her feet barely touching the floor.

"Come alone at sunset. Or she dies," his sire read and let out a heavy sigh. "I understand why you want to rush off, but you have to be smart about this. Getting yourself killed won't help her."

Just the other day, Odessa had said something similar to him. They were both right. In his current state, he'd never beat Claude, and it wasn't just his life on the line. It didn't mean he couldn't. He just had to play at all of his newfound strengths. And stop allowing his uncle to use his emotions as a weakness. Hamilton stared at Theo, the male who'd made him a vampire. Except he wasn't just any normal vampire. He was a hunter who'd transitioned into one. It was beyond time he started acting like it. Hamilton yanked his jacket off his shoulders and turned to the right.

"What are you doing?"

He glanced over his shoulder at his sire. "Accepting my truth." With that said, he strutted through the door leading down to the training room. There were some things he needed to collect.

Odessa eyed the ropes tied around her wrists. Not that she could see every detail all that well. Maybe if she tried another angle. Bending her head to the left, she scrutinized how they hung on the metal hook attached to the ceiling. With her tiptoes, she moved forward a touch and tried to rub the thick cord against the hook. Fuck. That didn't help. The ropes didn't even fray a little.

Sweat drenched her hair and forehead and trickled over her eyebrow. Blinking the bead from her eye, she rubbed her face against the thin sleeve of her shirt. There had to be a way to get out of here.

How long had she even been here? Inside this run-down apartment, or at least what remained of it. Although the water-stained ceiling held its own, the crusty paint had peeled, and the wallpaper rippled. From the appearance of this place, no one lived here. For all she knew, the building was condemned. The grime covering the windows and rusted grates made it impossible to determine her current location.

No décor of any kind existed in this room, which gave her nothing to go on. It looked like nothing more than an empty bedroom with an air conditioning unit that didn't function. Though no voices came through the thin wall, she heard footsteps shuffling along the hallway. Or so she assumed. "Hello?" Odessa called out.

A nearby door scraped against the floor and shut. Oh, God. Had Hamilton come to rescue her? "Hello? Hamilton?" *Please, let it be him,* she thought. It was the only option that boded well for her.

Heavy footsteps approached. Someone pushed the warped door open, which squeaked as it swung back. "Afraid not." Claude snickered.

"Let me go." The demand had come out before she could stop it. He didn't fear what Hamilton would do to him. And he'd already stripped her of all of her weapons, plus her shoes. How did she fight back with no help?

The male strode forward and smirked. "Why would I do that? You've already proven what side of this war you're on. What kind of hunter would I be if I didn't address that?"

"A smart one. Or is everything simply black and white to you?" His choice of clothing answered her question, but she posed it anyway. Like all the other hunters she'd crossed paths with, Claude donned black BDU's. Two blades rested crisscross across his back. From where she hung, she identified at least two other blades on his person—one at his right hip and the other against his left leg.

"Hunters have a code. We follow that code…without question. It's that simple."

"Is that why you sent a couple of fauns after us?" The more questions she asked, the longer she could delay whatever he had planned. It wasn't much, but she had to stall any way she could.

"I see Hamilton finally did as he was told and taught you something about hunters. Too bad it came a little too late." He snorted and strode closer to her. "But I'll happily answer you, Odessa. I didn't send them to fight you or kill him. I sent them to kidnap you. Just like I did with Einarr and Fortin. You can imagine my surprise when I see you and my nephew return to your apartment. I suppose that's what I get for underestimating your…dedication. Not a mistake I made a second time."

"Me? Why?" The photographs he'd left in that motel room made sense. He'd followed her to get to Hamilton. Except he had pictures of both of them. How did it all fit together? This couldn't be his first opportunity to get Hamilton alone.

"Because you, my dear, are his weakness. You always have been. It wasn't enough to work months on end, making all of this happen, leading us to this very moment. I had to allow him to have you, even just for a few days. So that when I ripped you from him, he'd jump without thinking. Of course, that also meant I had to get you here. Now, that took some calculated work, but I accomplished everything I set out to do. This won't be any different." Claude unsheathed the blade at his hip. "You will lead to his end." He dug the dagger's tip into her upper arm and sliced diagonally.

Odessa cried out in agony. Motherfucker! Shit. She had to say something or ask another question. Anything to get him to stop. Blood seeped through her shirt and trickled down her arm. "Why…?" she swallowed to wet her parched throat. "Why are you doing this?"

"His love for you makes him weak. His need to rescue you will be…a distraction. Not that he'll be able to find you." Claude punctured her thigh with the dagger and dragged it diagonally.

She screamed. It was like fire speared her leg, racing through her veins as if it had nowhere else to go. The ache in her shoulders intensified as her blood seeped through her clothes. Odessa's head lolled to the side. "You're wrong," she croaked out.

His footsteps carried across the floor. He returned a moment later and placed an empty bucket against the back of her feet.

"What the hell are you doing?" a male voice hollered from the doorway. "This isn't what we discussed."

Her gaze lifted to the blond-haired male as he grabbed Claude's arm.

The guy looked familiar, but she couldn't immediately place him. Not anyone she knew directly, but maybe through Hamilton. Fuck, it was getting hard to concentrate.

"*She…*," Claude pointed at her, "is a sympathizer. Our code strictly states we don't tolerate them. So, whether we discussed it is irrelevant. You'll do as I say." He growled. "Now, when the bucket is a third of the way full, take it and spread her blood throughout the building. Understood?"

"Yes, sir," the male grumbled.

"Good. I'm going to get ready for our guest." With that, Claude left the bedroom.

A minute later, the front door scraped against the floor and shut. Odessa fought against the weight holding her down. She couldn't let the darkness win. Her eyes shifted toward the rope and then fell to the bucket. Breaking the line may not work, but it didn't mean she couldn't do anything. She swung her left foot back and knocked the metal container over, spilling what blood had collected all over the dirt-streaked carpet.

"Shit," the male muttered. He rushed over to the bucket and picked it up. Letting out a heavy sigh, he scrubbed a hand down his face. "I'm really sorry about this, Odessa."

"Liar," she choked out. It didn't make a difference that he'd spoken as if he knew her. A person with any kind of moral compass wouldn't do this. Not that she had the strength to tell him such. Her eyelids drooped, and the room went pitch black as the abyss swallowed her whole.

Hamilton stared at the dilapidated building in front of him. Of all the addresses for Claude to give him, it had to be one directly across the street from Odessa's apartment. Although he'd never paid much attention to this eyesore, it didn't surprise him. His uncle had been under their noses the entire time.

He gripped the hilt of the sword hung on his hip. Before he'd left the manor earlier, he'd swapped out his Sebastian Cruz suit for a pair of tactical pants and a t-shirt. Then he strapped on a Katana, two scimitars crisscrossed across his back, and two daggers. One attached to his left thigh and the other in his right shitkicker. It didn't take anything special to kill a hunter. Any bit of steel would do the trick.

Summoning his invisibility, he peered at the double doors, one hanging off its hinges. He'd already scouted the alleys on either side of the building. Aside from the occasional rat scurrying along, he hadn't noticed anything. Even the first-floor windows hadn't offered him much in the way of information. At least nothing more than this was a condemned apartment building.

If someone planned construction or demolition, it hadn't yet begun. Hopefully, there weren't any squatters. Fewer witnesses he had to fret over. Knowing his uncle, this place would be completely devoid of life. Hamilton tightened his grip on the hilt of his Katana and slowly unsheathed it. Taking calculated steps forward, he grabbed the door handle and inched the good side open. He didn't have to control the circumstances to control the outcome.

The musty scent of mold and the coppery tang of blood assaulted his nostrils as he slipped inside. Hamilton clenched his jaw and white-knuckled the hold he had on his sword. His uncle had dared to harm Odessa. While a part of him wanted to race to her, the other part recognized the ignorance of that move. It was exactly what Claude expected him to do, which meant he had to do the opposite. He had to find his uncle first and rid the man of his head. Then he could go after Odessa.

The remnants of a security desk sat to his left. It was riddled with so many bullet holes it made Swiss cheese look good. That didn't include the holes in the wall behind it, letting him see the barren office. They should definitely demolish this place. He scoured the rest of the front entrance, but nothing appeared out of place. Debris covered the floor. All the ugly paintings along the wall hung askew. The elevator was clearly broken. And rust coated the nearby mailboxes. His ears twitched as he focused on the sounds. No matter how desolate the building looked, his uncle lurked around here somewhere.

Hamilton picked up the faint shuffle of footsteps toward the back of the building. Silently, he advanced down the hallway. Colorful graffiti covered the wall; a mix of tags and racial slurs. Passing by several apartment doors with missing doorknobs, he headed in the noise's direction. As he rounded the corner, the hall ended with the pool to the left and gym to the right. Someone had almost completely shattered the glass door leading to the gym. Not that the door to the pool had fared much better.

He glanced from one to the other. His uncle skulked in one of them. But which one? The lack of chlorine lingering in the air suggested the pool had long ago dried out. It would offer a few good hiding places for Claude, except that hadn't been the male's style. Proceeding forward, Hamilton carefully stepped over the gym door's metal frame.

"I'm so glad you finally showed up," Claude smirked and swung the silver blade in his hand around in a circle with a loud swoosh. "I almost thought you didn't care about your precious Odessa."

Last time they fought, he played right into his uncle's hands by reacting and responding to the guy's words. This time, he remained quiet. Hamilton shifted a few feet to the right, getting closer to Claude with each step.

"Your powers won't help you, nephew. Just because I can't see you doesn't mean I can't smell you. Your stench carries on the air like a disease that just won't go away."

Did the male think that would affect him? He'd heard his father use the same banter multiple times prior to his death. All vampires stink. At least in the eyes of a hunter. Instead of responding, he closed the distance between them.

Claude stepped to the left, swung his blade in a circle, and rested his hand on his hip. "Nothing to say? I expected more after everything I've done. That's alright. I don't really care to hear your last words." He threw a shuriken at Hamilton, who quickly dodged the small piece of silver, and brought his Katana down toward his uncle's head.

The male parried his attack. Their blades clanged as they came together. Last time they fought, this was where he messed up. He'd dropped his invisibility. That wouldn't happen this time. It would force Claude to use the extraordinary hearing he had.

Withdrawing, Hamilton feigned an assault from the right and struck his uncle from the left. He sliced the guy's arm. Blood splattered across the dirty floor as he ripped a part of his uncle's black shirt. One small strike, but their fight had only just begun.

The scent of Odessa's blood grew stronger. Not that it seemed possible. He hadn't seen her anywhere around the gym. Or close by. Unless Claude had dumped her in an apartment on the first floor. He'd gone right by them earlier. No. He would've noticed her natural smell lingering around any of those doors. His uncle wouldn't have left her somewhere he could find her first.

The odor overwhelmed him, which meant she had to be nearby. Except he couldn't catch a hint of her sweet aroma in the air. That could only mean one thing. Hamilton's eyes narrowed. Her injuries were far worse than he imagined. Shit. Shit. If her blood seeped from any of the floors above…it was the only thing that made sense.

He couldn't let Claude get away, but he couldn't let her die. *Hold on, Dess. I'm coming for you,* he thought. Although it wasn't a power either of them had, he got the sense she heard him. Or so he hoped. It was time to end this.

Hamilton lunged forward, swinging his blade over his head. His uncle deflected his attack, not that it stopped him from coming. Their swords repeatedly clanged together with each dodge. The longer the fight went on, the more irritated he became regarding his lack of knowledge about Odessa's safety. Pressing his blade close to the hilt of his uncle's sword, he knocked it out of the male's hand and swiped him across the face.

It gave him a chance—agony, like nothing he'd ever felt before, pierced his heart, forcing him to stumble backward a few steps. He briefly lost control of his invisibility. For a split second, he almost believed Claude had stabbed him. Except the male was too busy unsheathing scimitars from his back. Hamilton rubbed at his chest, attempting to ease the burning ache that had set up shop inside his heart, and disappeared out of sight.

God, please don't let it be Odessa.

Quietly slipping into the shadows, Hamilton steadied his breath, closed his eyes, and concentrated on every little sound around him. A faucet dripping in the locker room on the other side of the gym. Someone's feet clattering as they descended a nearby staircase. The resolute thrum of another's heartbeat—a sound that came from the same location. It couldn't be Odessa's heart. Not with the amount of blood he'd caught a whiff of.

He couldn't hear a damn thing from her. Not even a whimper. His eyes snapped open as something whooshed through the air. Hamilton sidestepped, but not fast enough. A blade struck his right biceps. Grabbing the hilt, he yanked it out and tossed it aside. It landed on the ground, skittering across the floor. Rage like he'd never known before consumed him. A red shadow flashed before his eyes.

Tightening the grip he had on his Katana, he dropped his invisibility, let loose a deafening roar, bared his fangs, and charged at Claude. Hamilton feigned an attack to the right, then darted to the left and swung upward, chopping off one of his uncle's hands. The scimitar in it hit the floor with a loud clank. The male howled in pain and staggered backward a few steps.

"Is that the best you've got?" Claude hollered through gritted teeth. He swiped at Hamilton with the scimitar in his other hand.

Hamilton parried, spun around, and drove his blade into the male's chest. Not that he'd hit the heart, but that was on purpose. His uncle deserved to feel every bit of torment possible as he delivered on his promise. Facing the male, Hamilton smirked as Claude hiccupped blood.

As much as he wanted to cut the male's head off, he had to institute justice first. His uncle dropped the scimitar, lurching on his feet. Hamilton slashed the guy across the throat. "That's for my father."

"You're weak," Claude said, his voice cracked. He coughed up more blood. "Always have—"

Before his uncle could get another word out, he swung his Katana and separated the male's head from the rest of his body. The head rolled as the body crumpled to the floor. The shuffling of footsteps on the other side of the gym caught his attention. Hamilton spun around on the back of his heel and threw a dagger through the air, burying it into the shoulder of his uncle's accomplice.

He raced across the room at extensive speed, slammed the male against the wall, and pressed the edge of his blade to the guy's neck. Hamilton stared at the blond-haired male. Of all the people to come after him, it shouldn't surprise him that included his best friend. Another hunter. He couldn't take the chance they'd come after him or Odessa again.

"Wait!" Asaph dropped his sword, letting it clatter to the floor, and held his hands up as if he'd accepted defeat. "Don't kill me! I'll tell you where Odessa is! I'll do whatever you want."

Two options stared him in the face. They each had their own downfalls. If he let his former best friend go, the male could return with other hunters to finish the job. But what if Odessa had little time left, and he wasted it scouring this building for her? "Where is she? I'll let you go, but you need to tell me her location now!"

"Fourth floor. Apartment four-oh-eight."

Hamilton released his hold on Asaph, who landed on the ground with a slight thump. He grabbed the hilt of his dagger still buried in the guy's shoulder. "Just so we're clear…any hunters who show up in my city *will* meet their end. In the same way as Claude. Got it?" Ensuring Asaph understood his meaning, he dug the dagger in a little.

The guy cried out in agony. "I got it!" he hollered.

"Good." Hamilton yanked the blade out and took off toward the stairwell. It was the fastest route to get to the floor he needed. The amount of blood he saw smeared across each step worried him. Please, just don't let him be too late.

He took care of his silver poisoning as he raced down the corridor.

Without a second thought, Hamilton threw open the apartment door Asaph had given him. The thick scent of fresh blood nearly knocked him off his feet. *Oh, God.* It was all Odessa's. And there was so much of it. Breathing through his mouth, he pushed forward and stormed through the apartment. The floor creaked with each step he took, not that he gave a shit. He had to find—

"Odessa," he choked out. "Oh, God." A deep crimson color caked her arm and leg. Her body dangled from a large hook as her head lolled to the side.

Tears welled in the corners of his eyes. Hamilton crossed the room in three long strides. He lifted Odessa from the metal piece connected to the ceiling. Holding her tight in his arms, he crouched down on the floor. "Please, please, please, come back to me," Hamilton whispered through soft sobs against her hair. Biting his wrist open, he pressed it to her lips.

Oh, God. Please, please, please…

No part of her responded. She didn't drink and didn't stir. There was no air in her lungs. Not even the faintest sound of her heart beating. This couldn't be happening. He couldn't have arrived too late. He couldn't have lost her. This couldn't be the end for them. "Please don't leave me," he whimpered.

Silence surrounded them.

Everything he'd fought for…it was all for nothing. Clutching Odessa's limp body against his chest, Hamilton screamed. The entire apartment shook. All the windows exploded; shards of glass rained down around them.

It didn't matter that he'd defeated Claude. Nothing in this life mattered. Not with Odessa gone.

ODESSA BOLTED UPRIGHT. SHE WINCED and pressed the heel of her palm to her forehead. Her head throbbed. It almost felt like someone drove a nail into her brainstem. That didn't include the pounding behind her eyes. Or the burning sensation coursing through her veins. Fuck. What happened? Why was the light so bright? "Oh, God," she groaned.

"Hey, hey, take it easy."

"Hamilton?" Cracking open an eye, she glanced around the room. Except she couldn't make anything out. It was all blurry. Oh, God. The throbbing in her head heightened. In a matter of seconds, it had gone from a minor thump to something closer to a jackhammer. Almost as if someone had started construction on her brain.

"Yeah, babe, it's me. You should lay back down. It'll make all of this a little easier." Taking her hand in his, he squeezed it and urged her to lie back.

"I don't understand," Odessa muttered. The back of her head hit the feathery pillow. Not that it made much of a difference. If anything, the drilling in her head got worse.

Hamilton let out a heavy sigh and brushed a kiss across the back of her knuckles. His lips were silky smooth and warm against her flesh. "You're transitioning."

"What?" What was he talking about? Transitioning into what? Her ears twitched at a bird trilling outside the window. "Make it stop." With her free hand, she pushed her palm against her temple. Fuck, that didn't help.

"Hold on." He stood and crossed the room.

She heard every hurried step he took. The gentle pit-a-pat of his shoes as it hit the carpet. How was that even possible? How could she hear the sounds so crisply? Oh, God. His words. She was *transitioning.* His blood. He'd used it to heal her…did that mean? Her mind reeled as the blaze in her veins intensified. It felt like a fire igniting inside her body. Tears stung the corners of her eyes.

"I'm so sorry, Dess. I swear to you I tried to prevent this," Hamilton said as he returned to her side. "I'm sorry I wasn't fast enough." He pressed another tender kiss to the back of her hand. "This is going to get painful, but I'll be here with you the entire time."

"It's okay," she croaked out. Her voice sounded rough. Like she'd gargled gravel. Was that part of the change? Or just from everything else going on in her body? Odessa opened her mouth, but nothing came out. Pure agony wracked her body. She curled up into a ball, which helped a little. The answers weren't important right now. They waited for her on the other side. Not that it mattered. She'd known the risks when she drank his blood. They both did. It was why he'd paused before giving it to her. Allowed her the opportunity to back out. Not that she'd change that decision. Even with these consequences.

The pit of her stomach rolled. The fire inside of her grew hotter. Odessa clenched her fists, digging her nails into the palm of her hands. She whimpered at the pain galloping across every nerve, lighting up every synapse like her body was the transition's own personal dance floor. Fuck. This was *seriously* going to hurt.

"I can give you some morphine…if you want. It won't help entirely, but it might help a little."

"No," she replied through gritted teeth and flopped over onto her back. Even if it offered some aid, she didn't care. She'd never depended on drugs to help with any of the pain she'd experienced in her life. She refused to start now. No matter how bad this got.

"Alright. Do you want to squeeze my hand?"

"Don't…want…to…break…it…" she got out between breaths. Sweat bloomed on her forehead. Fuck. Her back arched as she balled the bedding up in her hands. Every part of her skin crawled. All she wanted to do was rip it all off.

"I don't care if you do." He clasped one of her hands. "You squeeze however hard you need. I'll heal."

It was too late to argue. Odessa clutched his palm, gripping it tightly. The slight crunch barely registered as pangs of emptiness knotted her stomach and speared through the rest of her body. She screamed and writhed in agony. She didn't know how long this would last, but at least she had Hamilton right here with her.

Through every part of it. **For the rest of their** lives.

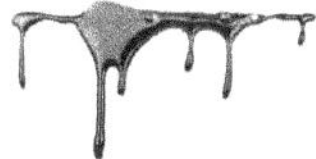

"I'm going to dry you off now." Hamilton gently wrapped a towel around Odessa, carefully lifted her out of the shower, and brushed a soft kiss on her forehead. She'd gotten through the transition beautifully. Though it had taken longer than his own as far as he remembered. The pain could take over.

"Skin…sensitive," she whispered.

"I know. It'll be like that for a while, but not forever." Maybe a few weeks, if he recalled correctly. That applied to all of her senses. As things improved, she'd get accustomed to all the changes that came with vampirism.

"Great," Odessa mumbled.

Hamilton snickered. He eased her onto the sink counter. "I'm sorry. I know this shouldn't amuse me, yet I can't help it." Not that he ever imagined this as a possibility between them. Since his transition, he'd always figured he'd locate a cure, and they'd come together as they once had. Now, everything was different.

"Jerk."

"I deserve that." Slowly, he unwrapped the towel from around her and used another one, delicately drying her off. Normally, he would've approached this from the top down, but it seemed like a better idea to go backward. Hamilton began with her feet and worked his way up toward her hair. Once he finished, he crossed the bathroom and retrieved a black-silk bathrobe from the hook. "This will be easiest for you to wear right now. All you need to do is just rest. Okay?"

"Yeah. Sleep sounds good."

"I'm sure it does." Transitioning into a vampire took a lot out of a person. Exhaustion setting in didn't surprise him in the least bit. While she slept, he could handle the last of everything with Claude's body. Before he'd left the building with Odessa in his arms, he'd planned to search every apartment. His uncle had likely stashed something there that might be of use to them. Even with the male now dead.

He got Odessa in the robe, scooped her up, sliding his arm under her knees, and carried her over to the bed. She'd already fallen asleep. Her eyes had drifted shut. And her chest gently rose and fell. She looked positively exquisite. Hamilton laid her down on the bed, stroked her cheek with the back of his knuckles, and pressed a loving kiss to her lips.

As he'd done earlier, he dug into his dresser and pulled out a pair of black tactical pants and a black t-shirt. He would've put on a suit, but this seemed more appropriate. Especially for the type of work on his plate. Hamilton dressed quickly, kissed Odessa one last time, and left the bedroom. He quietly descended the stairs, heading toward the library. That's where his sire's voice carried from. But who was the male speaking with?

"Are you certain this was necessary?"

"It is not something we could've helped. Though I believe it follows the prophecy to a tee."

Prophecy? What the fuck were they talking about? He lingered on the bottom step. From here, he could hear everything. Something about the other male's voice sounded recognizable. Was it someone he knew?

"There is no way to know that," Theo said. "Not with what little we understand about it."

"Then perhaps it is time we invite your newling into the room. Won't you join us, Hamilton?" the male called out.

Of course, the guy knew he stood there listening. Someone had told this male something about him. Was it one of the council members? Maybe Sebastian, the way his sire deferred to him. Hamilton stepped off the stair, crossed the foyer, and entered the library. He halted just inside the doorway and folded his arms across his chest. Something about the dark-skinned male seemed familiar, but he couldn't place him. Not necessarily the face, but definitely the voice. He'd heard it before.

"How is your fiancée?" his sire asked.

"Resting," Hamilton stated. He'd only answered out of politeness. The conversation he'd walked in on mattered more. As well as identifying the other male. He glanced between the two of them. "It seems I'm at a bit of a disadvantage. You know me, but I don't know you."

"Sebastian McCrae, at your service." He bowed to Hamilton with a slight flourish. "Though, I'm certain that is not all you wish to know."

How did he know that voice? They'd never met before. Of that, he was certain. Maybe if he got the male talking more, he could figure it out. "You're right. What's the prophecy?" It wasn't the only question he had, but it seemed the most important. At least until he got that bit of information.

"Here." Sebastian gestured to the open book on a nearby pedestal. "Look for yourself."

Yeah, he'd do that. Hamilton strolled over to the tome and scanned over the two pages. The left side referenced vampire beginnings. No specifics. But the other page offered something more. Not that he could make much sense of it. He read it again.

One born of the second sunlight
Thrives under the turn of night
Another born of the fourteenth day
Falls before the dawn
Their fates be intertwined
Setting the course for a new line
A strength unknown to mankind
As foretold by midnight

He lifted his gaze from the book and eyed them both. "And neither of you have any idea what it means?" Hamilton scrolled through the text a third time. Just in case he missed something.

"We believe it has something to do with you and your fiancée," Theo offered. "Though nothing more."

Why didn't he fully believe that? If it had something to do with him and Odessa, then it made sense they were the ones who investigated it. Provided they'd agree with his decision. "I take it you've both gone through this tome? Perhaps even others?"

"Yes," Sebastian responded. "It's why I was away when the council summoned you. Yet, we have discovered little to its meaning. Unless we take it at its word, which makes no sense given you're both now vampires."

Right. They couldn't reproduce. And what did midnight have to do with it? Hamilton opened his mouth and snapped it shut. His gaze flicked from Sebastian to the prophecy and back again. Son of a bitch. *That's* why the male seemed familiar. Sebastian was the vampire that had followed Odessa. But why? Unless…he glanced at the prophecy one last time. Even if it had everything to do with this, he couldn't react. There was far too much he didn't understand. Instead, he replied as if he hadn't figured it out, "Maybe it doesn't apply to us then. Either way, it would give us something to look into."

"I'm certain we could arrange that. Once she's gotten accustomed to her new powers, of course." Sebastian agreed and focused his attention on

Theo. "Do you concur?"

"Of course."

"Of course," Hamilton echoed. They'd accepted his suggestion way too easily. He and Odessa were very capable, more-so together. They'd find out everything these two **hid from them. One** way or another.

"You found all of this stowed away in that empty apartment building?" Odessa questioned as she scanned the many photographs she had spread across her mattress. They'd spent the last couple of days packing up her apartment. Only a few things remained. Given their distrust of Theodore and Sebastian, it made sense for them to discuss this here. But some of these pictures didn't look as if they belonged. A few of what she scanned were of Hamilton and the front gate of the mansion where they stayed.

"He was definitely here longer than either of us imagined. This is only just a small sample. I've got the rest hidden for now. Once we get moved into the new place, I'll collect them."

"Do you know who any of these people are?" She only recognized a couple faces aside from hers and Hamilton's. Yeah, according to these pictures, Claude spent around six months or longer in town.

"Yeah. And they worry me." Hamilton flipped through several of the pictures and pointed out four total. "These are three members of the council. I met them almost two weeks ago. And this one…this was the conservator on my staff before you."

Something Claude said to her came rushing back. "Oh, my God," she mumbled. "It makes so much sense now."

"What does?"

"Your uncle told me that everything he'd done wasn't enough. This was all part of his plan. Each photograph is only a small portion of every step Claude took to get us to that building." Odessa ran a hand through her hair and leaned back against the headboard. "It might take us a while to sort through everything, but if he followed members of the council…there's no telling what we might discover." They had to be extremely careful in how they handled their research and what they identified. Maybe some of it could help them decipher the prophecy he'd shared with her. And the reason Sebastian had followed her a few weeks back.

Hamilton scrubbed a hand across his face. "What do we do with this? Do we use it? Hide it?"

"For now, the latter." She collected them all into a pile and stuffed them in a manila envelope. "We're going to have to play by their rules. Follow their expectations and interact on their level." And she knew just how they started. This was going to suck for both of them. Odessa climbed off the bed and clasped Hamilton's hand within her own. "We'll have to set the stage. Beginning with our wedding. I know neither of us wanted anything extravagant, but…we need to use their weaknesses against them." And grow stronger at the same time. He'd told her the council had special powers. They'd have to figure out how to prevent them from being used on either of them.

"Please tell me you're joking."

"I never joke about ass-kissing." She pushed up on her tiptoes and brushed a soft kiss across his lips. "Now come on, we've got a lot of work to do. And since you're presenting me to the council tomorrow, I need to find the perfect dress."

"You're killing me, Dess. You're killing me."

"It should be quite the opposite, my dear." Odessa snickered. "I'm impressing you." At least everything she'd learned about high society as a child would finally pay off. Although, years had gone by since she'd executed an appropriate curtsy. She might wish to practice before they left the apartment tonight.

"You always do that." He picked up the manila envelope as her cell phone rang. Hamilton raised an eyebrow.

Odessa checked the caller ID. "My father." Leaving her bedroom, she stepped away to answer the call. "Hi, Papa." It was smarter to leave him behind, but she couldn't break his heart. Not yet. They'd agreed to give her father and brother some time before faking her death. This way, they'd keep them both away from New York. With all the work now laid at their feet, this was definitely the best way to go.

One day, it would all be over.

Then they could start somewhere new without looking back.

Hamilton stared at Odessa. He couldn't help it as her expressions shifted on their approach to the mansion. It went from shock to awe and then back again. The navy-blue full-length gown she'd selected for her presentation complemented her alabaster skin beautifully. It made her light up. He even like the flowy skirt and floral appliques that covered it. Though he'd half-expected her to come out in something black or orange. It was Halloween. Not that vampires celebrated the holiday. All Hallows Eve belonged to the witches.

Odessa glanced between him and Theodore, who sat in the front passenger seat. "Don't suppose they have a ballroom here?"

"Yes, Miss Black," he replied as the car slowed to a stop.

Hamilton smirked. Why would she ask that? Did she have plans to suggest a masquerade or something? Odessa half-shrugged. They'd agreed to play a part. He might have to brush up a bit more before attending anything of that caliber. A moment later, his door opened, and he got out. He walked around the back of the car, opened the rear passenger side door, and held out his hand to her. His green eyes sparkled and a broad grin crossed his face as she slid her palm into his hand. "Have I told you lately how exquisite you look this evening?"

"Hmm? You may have said something about it. It certainly complements the jewelry you gave me." Not only had he given her a pair of dangling diamond earrings, but he'd *upgraded* her engagement ring, too. It was now over three karats in a platinum setting. "Though I'm curious when you had time to pick it all out."

"Having Grayson around has its perks." He offered her his arm and escorted her to the front door. Although she'd attempted to keep the dress from his sight, he'd snuck a peek. The rest he simply couldn't resist.

"I imagine it does." Odessa flashed a bright smile at him, lighting up as the front door opened wide.

Maybe he was biased, but the council was going to love her. She fit into this world better than he did. Not just high class either. These last few days she'd taken to vampirism with great ease, almost how she handled learning a new language. It fit her beautifully. Something he couldn't wait to see more of. Her fingers curled around his arm, tightening slightly as they headed inside. Hamilton led her down the hall of paintings toward the study.

"Who are these people?" she whispered.

"You'll see." He dipped his chin at the set of double doors at the end of the hall. Voices carried even in hushed tones in this house. No reason to offer details he'd shared with her the other day.

"Understood."

Together, they strode through the heavy oak doors. The clicking of Odessa's high heels heightened as they headed to the room's center. Her eyes brightened as she drank in the sizeable library behind the council seats. He watched as Isaac and Devereaux both sat up a little straighter. Sebastian smirked and steepled his fingers together. None of the other males reacted, not that he expected that would last.

Hamilton's ears perked up as his sire and Grayson joined them. The doors closed a moment later. He bowed his head to the council. "My lords. I present to you Miss Odessa Black."

Odessa unfurled her fingers from his arm and lowered her head to the council as she gripped the sides of her dress. She shifted her right foot and executed a perfect court curtsy, dropping close to the floor. Even from where he stood, he noticed a few more of the males practically salivating. His fiancée absolutely knew what she was doing, especially as she rose to her feet.

Isaac stood, climbed down from the ceremonial stage he sat on with the council, and crossed the room with a few long strides. The male bowed to Odessa, lifted her hand, and pressed a kiss to the back of her knuckles. "Miss Black, you are quite the specimen. Welcome to our ranks."

"Thank you, my Lord," she replied.

As the male rose to his full height of nearly seven feet, his gaze flicked to Hamilton. "Though, I assume you brought more than something so precious to your accompaniment."

"Of course." With a quick nod to their butler, he clasped his hands behind his back. As they'd discussed the day before, Grayson walked around them and laid out three burlap bags on the floor. They had blood speckled along the bottom, but he couldn't help that.

Isaac narrowed his mahogany eyes. "Impressive. We request one and you bring us more."

"I didn't wish for them to go to waste." It had occurred as an afterthought. He'd initially planned to burn all the bodies until Theo suggested otherwise. How could he pass up the chance to deliver such a wonderful message to the council?

"No, of course not," Isaac commented. He flicked his wrist and a nearby servant hastily collected the bags from the floor. "Nothing should ever go to waste." The male exchanged a glance with the council members and focused back on Hamilton and Odessa. "This calls for a celebration. Though we cannot put anything proper together in such a short time, perhaps you would consider joining us for dinner."

"I'm quite amenable to that." Odessa beamed at Hamilton. "If you are, *my love.*"

God, he loved her with every bone in his body. Not that he'd ever thought two emphasized words could sound sexier. He couldn't help the glint in his eyes as he grinned widely at his fiancée. Hamilton lifted her hand, kissed the top of it, and curled it around his arm. "Whatever you desire."

Odessa squeezed his biceps and flicked her gaze to Isaac. "Please, lead the way, my Lord."

"As you wish." Isaac dipped his chin at Odessa. He spun around on the back of his heel and nodded to the council. "Let us conclude this session and enjoy the rest of our evening."

Hamilton pressed a kiss to Odessa's temple as they strode forward. Wasn't this going to be interesting? And a hell of a lot different from sitting through a meal with Theo. At least he'd gotten accustomed to those over the last year. But it was a step in the right direction. Something they needed to uncover all the dirty secrets buried in the abyss the council had created. Even if they **had to get down in the** gutter to do it.

With ragged breaths, Odessa collapsed against Hamilton's chest. Holy shit. There were some amazing benefits that came with vampirism. While she didn't care all that much for the taste of blood, it certainly made sex *so* much better. "Amazing," she uttered. This had been a damn good way to break-in their new place.

"Yeah, it was," he said between heavy breaths. Hamilton swept her sweat-drenched hair aside, rolled her over, and tucked her into his side.

The fire crackled; slowly dying, it licked at the remnants of wood as if it hungered for more. Though she noticed the change in temperature, it no longer bothered her. Another perk of her new status. Odessa's attention left the opulent fireplace as she peered around the vast space of their penthouse suite. They hadn't brought in any furniture or boxes yet. None of that would happen until they handled the construction. She lifted her gaze to her fiancé.

"What are you thinking about?"

"All the work we still have to do in this place." Not that it really required it, but they had to create a safe space for their research. They'd already begun building their relationships with the individual council members.

"Is that a statue of Amphitrite?" Odessa asked as Devereaux led them into a large room full of statues and paintings.

"Yes, it is. Most people get that wrong." He tilted his head at her. *"How did you know?"*

"Greek mythology has always fascinated me, so I learned how to recognize the gods and goddesses at a young age. It's actually part of what led me into my field." She eyed the various pieces he had displayed across the room. It seemed split into a few different parts, though all of it was Greek. *"Given how vampires came into existence, I'm a tad surprised you've collected so much that strays from Christian beliefs."*

"I'm a conveyor of the arts, regardless of where it comes from."

"I imagine that leads to some interesting dinner conversations." Not that she'd noted anything off throughout their meal. Out of her periphery, Odessa glimpsed at Hamilton, who quietly straggled behind them. They'd decided a couple days ago that they'd accept any offer of a tour of the manor. It would help them later on down the line.

"Of course, a good debate over the fabrics of life makes for the best conversations."

"Yet, no one broached the topic regarding anomalies in myself and Hamilton. I know I haven't met many others, but I don't imagine it only exists in just us two." It went without saying she referred to their ability to consume food. Something Hamilton told her typically applied only to born vampires. Though her fiancé had great strength and speed, they hadn't determined if it made him more powerful than a birthed vampire.

Devereaux offered her a lopsided grin. *"You're correct, Miss Odessa. It is rare, however, you're not the only one."*

"Interesting. Has anyone researched what makes it possible? If it's something in our heritage or DNA that allows it." Or if the existence of one meant other anomalies existed, too. Not that she posed that question. It was best to keep some mystery to their conversation.

"Both Darian and Isaac have done their own individual research. It actually led to a conflict because neither could agree on the outcome."

That was interesting. Her gaze settled on a statue of Aphrodite. The goddess of love, beauty, and procreation. *"Perhaps they didn't go deep enough in vampiric history,*" *she suggested.*

"Hey, I know it seems like a lot, but we have to do whatever it takes to protect ourselves," Hamilton replied.

Odessa sat up a little and rested her chin on his chest. "Does that mean you still think letting that hunter go was a good idea?" Information he'd shared after she'd fully come around from her transition. Some part of her hadn't agreed with the decision. Not that either of them could change it. And that male had seemed a bit out of his element.

"It was a risk, but I believe it was the right move. He won't return." He brushed the back of his knuckles across her cheek. "We have enough to worry about without fretting over him."

"You're right." They had seven council members to schmooze. A world of classy vampires to infiltrate. A web of photographs to untangle. And a wedding to plan. All as they unraveled the meaning of that prophecy.

They required answers. No matter what it took or what they had to do. Together, they'd figure it out. As long as they had each other, no one could stop them.

The End
Or is it?

That is the question.

ABOUT THE AUTHOR

Author of the Love's Worth Series, BRIGIT ROSÉ, lives in a world of romance. She has taken her life experience and made it into one endless love story. When she's not writing, she's singing loudly and off-key, hanging out with friends, or playing with her 2.5 fur babies. She can usually be found with a kiss in one hand and a twist of lime in the other, exactly the stories she likes to read and write. If you'd like to know more about Brigit, you can find out more on her website:

KBFENNERROSE.COM

OTHER WORKS BY BRIGIT ROSÉ

LOVE'S WORTH SERIES
UnHinged
ReIgnited

THE LUCENT CHRONICLES
Grace's Beast

Under Krys Fenner

DARK ROAD SERIES
Addicted
Damaged
Avenged
Burned

THE GUARDHIAN SERIES
Awakened

Co-Authored

PRISMA ISLE SERIES
Perfectly Reckless
Chaotic Tranquility
Rebel Tides
Siren's Curse
Silencing the Shape Shifter

Insider's Guide
Prisma Isle Puzzle & Coloring Book

Coming Soon

Blood & Bondage (The Empyreal Den Chronicles)
Disillusioned (The Guardhian Series)
Inherited (The Guardhian Series)
Twisted (Dark Road Series)
Shattered Wonderland (The Lucent Chronicles)

*Keep reading for a preview
of Grace's Beast*

A "BEAUTY & THE BEAST" RETELLING
THAT APPEARS IN THE SAME WORLD

one

"THE ONE-STORY VICTORIAN-STYLE HOUSE ON Rose Hill that had once been full of life, joy, and love was eerily empty and lonely. All the family portraits had been removed from the walls in the living room, along the hallways, and from most of the bedrooms. Yet, none of the furniture had changed in any of the rooms."

"In the living room, the vanilla-colored walls hadn't been altered, nor had the charcoal-gray couch in the center of the room or the wide, cherry TV stand across from it. The queen-sized bed with a matching, traditional gray, four-piece bedroom set remained in the spare bedroom. A four-post bed with slated lines and time-honored silhouettes had lasted for years in the second bedroom. A matching dresser and nightstand finished in beautiful, antique black had outlasted the photographs as well."

"Even the master-bedroom had gone untouched. It had the same king-sized bed and antique-white, six-piece bedroom set the lovers once shared when they first moved into the house and turned it into a home. The only difference: it was now shrouded in darkness. All the light had been extinguished as if joy never existed in the first place."

"The lovers' only heir had chosen to live in isolation, with nothing to survive on but their memory."

Vincent's grip on his coffee mug tightened until his knuckles turned white. He cracked his neck and ground his teeth.

Nothing but their memory replayed in his mind. As if that was all his parents were. Just a memory.

Yes, they had been killed in a car crash nearly eleven years ago, but his parents meant more than just some cockamamie words on paper. Their story was more than whoever had written this…garbage! That's exactly what it was, pure and utter garbage. He didn't care how accurate the details were. His parents deserved more than what whoever had spewed this crap had given them.

That was the problem. He didn't know who had written this junk novel laid out before him.

The answer wouldn't be any different this time than it had been any other time since he had gone back to the front of the manuscript, but he did it again, anyway. Vincent stared at the space where "written by" should—no, would—have normally appeared.

Except there was nothing.

No "written by." No "by." Nothing to help him determine the novel's author. Of course, all of this had been on purpose. It was all part of the stupid competition his company ran annually. The one used to find new artists eager to have a publishing deal of any kind. Not that it was necessarily a poor offer: ten grand and a one book publishing contract. The first two authors they'd signed had seen splendid success. Not so much with the last one.

But of all the entries he had read, none of them had ever been a story about his family…his parents…him.

And this one was just that.

It was *his* story, which made it his responsibility to make sure it never saw the light of day. No matter what.

Vincent banged his fist on the polished cherry-oak desk and knocked the pen holder to the floor. Pens scattered across the plush, gunmetal-gray carpet. Yanking the phone from its cradle, he depressed the button for his assistant.

"Get in here, now!" he screamed into the line and slammed the phone back down. Shit, he had to get himself under control. He couldn't let his other side come out. Inhaling and exhaling a couple of deep breaths, he mentally chanted the mantra *I am the calm before a storm.*

Burying his face into his hands, he groaned and dragged a hand through his dirty-blond hair. Vincent hung his head and gripped the back of his neck. He could easily stop this manuscript from going forward without having to find out who authored it.

No. He had to find out. Whoever had written this story knew too much about his heritage, and that left him vulnerable. He had to know who they were and how they had found out so much about his…abilities.

Vincent stood, rising to his full height. He straightened the deep-red tie at his throat, the black jacket across his broad shoulders, the black pants around his waist and crossed over to the view his office offered him of *the city*. His office sat a good hundred-feet high with a large bay window. From his vantage-point, he could see the white flakes as they danced across the sky and blanketed the ground. One of the many things he enjoyed about the winter months. The cooler air also felt good against his preternaturally warm skin. His internal temperature ran higher than a human's.

A minute detail the manuscript had gotten right.

There was a slight rap at the door to his office, and then it opened. "My apologies for my delay, sir. You requested my presence."

Lacing his fingers together behind his back, Vincent tracked the movements of the people he saw trekking through the snow-covered sidewalk below, likely in search of Christmas gifts. If he were human, the insignificant creatures going on about their insignificant lives would look like nothing more than black dots.

But he wasn't human. And the author behind the manuscript on his desk knew it.

It was against the rules to find out who authored a story, but he needed them broken. His life was more important than the rules. Vincent glanced over his shoulder. "Yes, I did. Louis, close the door."

"Yes, sir." His assistant shut the door, stepped further into the office and swallowed. He fidgeted with the pen and pad of paper in his hands. "Have I done something wrong?"

Vincent raised an eyebrow. What nonsense were fools in the office filling his assistant's head with now? Louis was the one person he trusted in this godforsaken building. Hell, in this city. Frowning, he turned to face him and crossed his arms. "Of course, not. I simply need you to do something."

"Oh, of course, sir. Whatever you need." Releasing a deep breath, Louis closed some of the distance between them, stopping to collect the pens on the floor and return them and the holder to the desk.

"Leave them." Vincent snarled. He'd deal with the pens later. Once his assistant dropped the pens, Vincent shifted his gaze toward the manuscript blatantly sitting on his desk. "I need you to…discreetly…find someone. And it's imperative you do it without question. Do you understand?"

Louis tilted his head. He glanced from Vincent to the manuscript on the desk and back again. "Oh! Um, yes, sir. Of course. As you wish."

"Thank you."

With a bow of his head, Louis fetched the manuscript from the large cherry-oak desk and paused halfway to the door. He looked back at Vincent. "Sir, this is—"

"Without question."

"But, sir—"

"Just do it." Vincent growled.

Louis gasped and scampered out of the office.

Vincent turned toward the window once again. His reflection stared back at him. Electricity pulsated behind his blue eyes. His jawline shifted. Even his canines elongated a touch. The monster started clawing its way out.

GRAB YOUR COPY
TODAY!